EXTRA INNINGS

ALSO BY

Robert Newton Peck

A Day No Pigs Would Die

Soup

A Part of the Sky

Nine Man Tree

Cowboy Ghost

EXTRA INNINGS

by Robert Newton Peck

HarperCollins*Publishers*

Extra Innings
Copyright © 2001 by Robert Newton Peck
All rights reserved. No part of this book may be used or
reproduced in any manner whatsoever without written
permission except in the case of brief quotations
embodied in critical articles and reviews.
Printed in the United States of America.
For information address HarperCollinsChildren's Books,
a division of HarperCollins Publishers,
1350 Avenue of the Americas, New York, NY 10019.
www.harperchildrens.com

Library of Congress Cataloging-in-Publication Data
Peck, Robert Newton.
Extra innings / by Robert Newton Peck.
p.   cm.
Summary: After a tragic airplane crash that claims the lives
of most of his family, sixteen-year-old Tate goes to live with
his wealthy great-grandfather and his adopted black great-aunt
Vidalia and he finds unexpected solace in the stories of
her childhood spent traveling with a Depression-era
Negro baseball team.
ISBN 0-06-028867-1 — ISBN 0-06-028868-X (lib. bdg.)
[1. Great-grandfathers—Fiction.   2. Great-aunts—Fiction.
3. Baseball—Fiction.   4. Family life—Southern States—Fiction.
5. Interracial adoption—Fiction.   6. Southern States—Fiction.]
I. Title.
PZ7.P339 Ex   2001
[Fic]—dc21   00-38875
1   2   3   4   5   6   7   8   9   10
❖
First Edition

In Gratitude

The author wishes to thank his teammates,
who so willingly played *Extra Innings*.

Vick Vickers,
who taught me how to fly an airplane.

Jon Rose,
my neighbor and friend,
who really knows baseball.

Hal Morris,
a good buddy,
who has played first base for the
New York Yankees, the Cincinnati Reds,
and also the Detroit Tigers.

—R.N.P.

EXTRA
INNINGS

STONEMASON
Family Tree

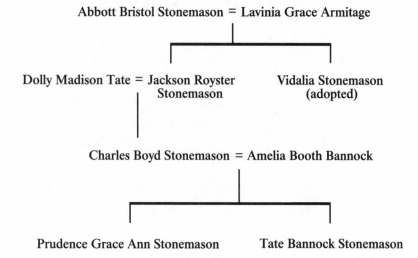

Abbott Bristol Stonemason = Lavinia Grace Armitage

Dolly Madison Tate = Jackson Royster Stonemason

Vidalia Stonemason (adopted)

Charles Boyd Stonemason = Amelia Booth Bannock

Prudence Grace Ann Stonemason

Tate Bannock Stonemason

PROLOGUE

A BONGO DRUM.

That's how the boom-boom-booming head of Pasquale Prieto was pounding, due to last night's cheap rum. Reeking of another woman's perfume, he had stumbled home drunk, inciting Yesenia and her bully of a brother to throw him, and his belongings, out of her trailer and into a rainstorm. Desperate for a place to sleep, he tried José's Mexican Cantina, even though it was self-described as "Florida's Bare-Fisted Bar."

"In here, any guy with two ears," José enjoyed informing his clientele, "is a poof."

A throat-scarred stranger, displaying an I LOVE MY MOTHER AND I'M GOING TO LOVE YOURS tattoo on his beefy biceps, bragged how he wasted Cubans; then proved it by smashing an empty bottle over Pasquale's skull.

Hours later, in wet clothes, slowly regaining consciousness on the shattered shards of glass in the alley, with cuts on his hands and too sick to eat breakfast, Pasquale discovered one more delightful surprise. His wallet was missing. Why hadn't he stayed in Miami, at his cousin's Little Havana duplex on

1

Southwest Sixth Street, several overpopulated blocks off Calle Ocho?

He groaned, *"Tonto."*

Stupid was surely the word.

An early sun's brightness warned his squinting eyes that he'd be late to his nothing job at a fixed-base operation. One more mistake and Pasquale Prieto, a newly hired plane servicer, would be booted out on his *arsenio*.

This was a major concern, because now he suddenly had become an undocumented illegal alien without a green card. And it would take time and money to obtain another fake one.

Arriving at the workplace he hated—a no-tower, uncontrolled airfield for small craft—Pasquale forced himself to report in, blinked briefly at the first assignment on his duty sheet, located keys, and started the fuel truck's motor. Chugging forward, the truck splashed through several large puddles left over from last night's storm. It bypassed an expensive Sabreliner jet and a more modest Beechcraft, marked as a Mexican XY-FCES.

He tried to think. Before fueling a plane, wasn't there something he ought to do first? Pasquale's foot stomped the brake.

"Sí."

A week ago, the boss, with a mouthful of doughnut, had mumbled his redneck English too fast, yet Pasquale recalled some of the confused instruction. He was supposed to drain a few gallons of fuel from the belly spigot below the truck's giant tank, to check for contamination such as grit, water, and trash—all of which settled to a tank's bottom and were easily detected. Doing so today, however, was a lot to expect from a hangover in a hurry.

Pasquale shrugged.

Fuel was usually okay. Besides, inhaling the direct fumes of avgas sometimes made him throw up. So, he decided, he'd save time and skip the mandatory inspection for fouled fuel.

Fighting nausea, Pasquale pumped gasoline into the gleaming white Cessna 421 with the blue identification on its tail.

N19SM

Twenty minutes later, a meticulously attired pilot approached to make preflight checks: tire condition, doors, engine oil, plus every exterior observation. As he returned inside the building to the fuel desk, a gray-uniformed chauffeur parked a white stretch limousine to disgorge a group of six passengers: grandparents, parents, plus a pair of spirited teenagers. Both doors, upper and lower, were quickly opened to allow them to board, as this entourage was hardly a family to be kept waiting. The girl, slightly older than her brother, waved a cheerful good-bye and blew a kiss to the smiling black driver, then occupied the right-forward seat, a copilot's location, had there been one.

Behind her, a foursome of adults faced one another, shuffled cards, and prepared to play bridge.

In the extreme rear, a beardless boy willingly volunteered to hunker down sideways on a flat single cushion, more or less facing the doors. Though it was the least-hospitable seat, the youngster's rapturous grin proclaimed that he didn't mind the cramped quarters, which were designed more for baggage than for people.

Why should he mind? After all, they were en route to Atlanta's new baseball facility, with box seats at a posh stadium, where the Braves would host the Rockies.

The family's personal pilot boarded, smiled, threw a crisp salute, and then crept along a very narrow center aisle to his left-forward position of command. Pleasantries were exchanged. He sat, belted, starting both 350 HP tri-prop engines and, once their six propellers spun a confident hum, dedicated himself to routine. Generator switch on. Electric load meters checked, along with both radios: Com 1, Com 2. He established navigation frequencies, Nav 1 and Nav 2. Verification included ADF, an automatic directional finder that was merely a local AM radio station, WCAT. Tanks, L and R, were monitored as well as fuel-selector switches.

Flight prep took three minutes.

The $300,000 swan smoothly glided onto the taxiway; on radio, the pilot announced his intentions for departure: "Cessna . . . November one niner Sierra Mike . . . taking runway two-one, right turnout, northbound."

A reply was neither received nor anticipated.

Once on the runway, the pilot advanced both throttles for takeoff, and N19SM (the final pair of letters representing the family's name, Stonemason) thrust into a light wind, accelerating, gracefully lifting off at 83 mph. Faster . . . faster . . . the plane pulsed with power.

But then, all went wrong.

The L engine severely vibrated, coughed twice, and abruptly quit, forcing the pilot to rudder, correcting for engine malfunction. Although the landing gear tricycle was not yet retracted, the plane had already devoured too much of the runway and was now totally committed to flight. The R engine sputtered and died. The Cessna's altitude was no more than twelve feet, and dead ahead, nothing but a stand of tall pines.

The pilot said two words: "Oh God."

As the young woman beside him gasped a silent scream, he attempted to steer the powerless aircraft between a pair of nearest trees. Airspeed read 81. In seconds, the L wing hit the first pine, jerking the plane's nose to the left. The opposite wing struck another stout, ruggedly barked trunk, snapping off the entire tail section.

The boy was thrown clear.

In less than a breath, a snarl of exposed electrical wires, or sparks from mangled metal scraping against metal, detonated the remainder of the disintegrating plane. It became a bomb. A monstrous and billowing orange cloud, exploding over two hundred gallons of highly volatile gasoline into a searing obliteration.

Mouth open, a trembling Pasquale Prieto witnessed the horror, said nothing, and hurriedly left for Miami.

BOOK I

TATE

1

"HURRY IT UP, YOU POKES."

Thirty feet behind, passing slowly beneath a gum tree, sixteen-year-old Tate wasn't spurred by the older man's gruffness. The spry gentleman of eighty-two had halted and turned to smile warmly at a great-grandson and a dog.

Close to Tate's side, Ballerina, the coonhound bitch, might have kept pace with their patriarch despite her age and hesitant gait. Yet, among the tall shafts of golden switch-grass she waited, to encourage the boy with her company.

Determined to endure the bellowing throb in his right leg, Tate marveled at her concern that he could no longer run. Barely walk. Six months ago, a crashing Cessna had annihilated his leg to within a prayer of amputation.

Tate had been the only survivor.

Six others died, consumed by exploding flame: the family's professional pilot; Tate's older sister, Prudence Grace;

9

and their parents and paternal grandparents.

After a week in shock, Tate could speak; it took a month to sit up in a hospital bed, two more months with crutches, and another six weeks hobbling on a cane. Today was Tate Bannock Stonemason's first hike among the familiar and fragrant pines and oaks of the family's far-flung Florida estate.

"Doing okay, Tater?"

"We're both coming, Great-Granddad."

Struggling forward, Tate stroked the hound's silky head. A dainty dog, Ballerina was sleek and slender, almost entirely black, with patches of brown over her intelligent eyes, on her jowls, and along her delicate legs. Eleven years ago, she had wandered to his great-grandfather's kitchen door, thin and hungry, too dignified to beg.

Aunt Vidalia had petted and fed her, named her Ballerina, and adopted her for life, as Vidalia herself had been permanently adopted and given the name Stonemason.

"She knows." The elderly man waited for them. "Had I brought the Purdey, she'd be ahead of us, Tater, quartering a field, inhaling information with every sniff, and flushing quail." Kneeling to cradle her chin in a gentle hand, he added, "Ballerina realizes we didn't bring a gun."

"At times," Tate admitted, "she's so clever it's spooky. When my laundry bag's full, she tugs at it with her teeth, telling me to tote it downstairs to the washer."

"Whip smart. If trailing a raccoon that takes to wet, she won't follow. In water, a coon'll drown a dog in seconds because under the surface, a lot of hounds are too stupid to hold breath. But no coon'll drown Ballerina." Bending to touch the moist ground with the tip of an arthritic finger, Great-Granddad said, "Bobcat track. No wonder our whooping cranes aren't so plentiful." He stood up, then pointed. "Look over yonder."

Tate squinted. "Whoopers?"

"No. Notice the bright red tufts on their heads? Sandhill cranes. And those longleggers way beyond are ironhead storks."

"If you say so."

Tate didn't know an ironhead from a Sopwith Camel. Yet he planned to learn. Trying to balance himself, he involuntarily yielded to his troubled leg and winced, aware that little escaped the steel-gray observation of Abbott Bristol Stonemason.

"Pain," his great-grandfather said compassionately. "Personal and private. Impossible to shoulder for another. A leg is the least of all yours." Again he caressed the coonhound. "We three are all suffering, Tate. This venerable hunter, her tail once high and happy, feels discomfort with every step. Going deaf. Sleeps indoors in patches of parlor sunlight to ease her stiffness." He studied her face. "Those eyes are a cloudy fog of winter, overcast, as if Ballerina's seen all that she was meant to see."

For an instant, Tate's pain eased in the pride of being the great-grandson of the stalwart yet sensitive man who now tousled his hair.

"Blessings," the old voice said, "far more than burdens have always been bestowed on me, Tate. When your great-grandma Lavinia was alive, we took little Viddy to our hearts and home. Over sixty years ago, it was unheard of for a white family to adopt color. And now you're also living with us."

"It's all so strange, Great-Granddad."

"Hope I survive long enough to fashion you some. Not into my mold. Into yours." He shook his head. "Enough sentiment. I can't stomach too much artificial sweetener. How's the leg?"

"Mending," he lied.

"Bully, as Theodore Roosevelt liked to say. Way before my time, but I read he was sickly but never a quitter."

"Is this a pep talk? Sorry, but I received too many from the hospital shrink, so pardon my being full up on motivation."

A.B. said, "Consider yourself pardoned. On that score, I hope you pardon Vidalia and me. Living with two elderly people may not be comfortable for you. Yet with us is where you belong. For now."

"You and Aunt Vidalia seem so formal."

"We're devotees of tradition. I would suppose it is just plain stuffiness."

"You and Aunt Vidalia are fingers on a fist. Both of you old-fashioned South."

"Viddy's a conservative lady and has always formed her own boundaries of propriety. Abhors trash, be it black or white. At times, she's an uppity snob." He held up a finger. "But her bias is based on conduct. Certainly not on wealth." The older man patted the dog. "Good grief, lad, Vidalia is seventy! At this age, do you imagine she's fixing to budge an inch? Not hardly. Our charming, caring, and often contrary matron is the most financially endowed heiress in Swamp County. Viddy has two stockbrokers, three savings accounts, plus bonds and a stack of tax-free municipals."

It pleased Tate to learn this. For years, his parents had told him that, when he first began to talk at age two, his first word was "Viddy." As he grew, Vidalia and he were woven by affection into a strange union, a combining that elated the entire Stonemason clan.

Great-Granddad said, "Yup. Her inheritance began even before your grandfather, Jackson Royster Stonemason, was born. Although obviously adopted, Vidalia was our first child and my only daughter. She's now quite comfortable off. Supports her church, the African Blood-of-the-Lamb Baptismal Chapel, the hospital, and a number of charitable organizations, including a library. You're aware she's well-read. Intellect is her better side." A.B. snorted, spat, and whispered a sorry word. "To annoy me, Miz Viddy's also a confounded Republican!"

Again he cussed.

Tate laughed at the bark-tough Democrat, and the coonhound wagged her tail, as if knowing how soft the aging atheist really was.

They strolled slowly through a stately stand of titanic camphor trees and some shorter wax myrtles, smelling the tart aroma.

"What was Vidalia like at ten?" Tate asked.

"A tiny woman. To a busload of colored baseballers, little Viddy served as both mascot and mother, or so Lavinia noticed. Called themselves Ethiopia's Clowns. Those gifted rascals were the only family she knew, and none of them were kin."

Gritting his teeth, Tate stepped over a fallen log, closing his eyes against the agony that cut into him. He was a trapped animal, a limb gripped by the iron teeth of tragedy. If he could only gnaw off his leg and escape.

In his mind he cupped a ball, feeling threads, right arm cocking like a coiling whip, able to fire a baseball over either corner of a white five-sided target sixty feet and six inches away. Fingertips caressed the endless seam, a curving serpent to present what every pitcher demands. Grip. For a moment, he was again at Callahoochee High School, where all eyes watched their sophomore sensation. Plus the experienced scrutiny of baseball scouts who were there only to see young Tate Stonemason throw, hit, bunt, slide, and steal bases. He could do it all.

His great-grandfather's grizzled voice bugled him home to reality. "Your face seems far away. You've left Ballerina and me to lonesome. Deep thoughts?"

"A few childish memories."

"Remember the good ones, Tater. A healthy mind is a photograph album, where only our joyous images are saved."

2

Dinner would be served at seven.

Before coming downstairs to the cheery, chandelier-lit dining room, Tate luxuriated with a hot shower, a shampoo, and a change into fresh clothes. He'd permanently moved in at Stonemason Manor, now occupying a spacious bedroom with clothes and possessions, most of which Aunt Vidalia had neatly arranged on shelves, in drawers and closets.

Both his parents had been killed, as well as his pal of an older sister, Prudy, so he couldn't live alone in their house.

Since early childhood Tate had dined weekly at the manor house of his great-grandfather, as did other Stonemasons of varying vintage. Before dinner, in years past, family members assembled in the library to rejoice with crackling fires in both fireplaces if cool weather demanded, one cocktail each for adults, served with Frederickson's white gloves and winsome smile.

Often there was a toast.

Crystal flutes of champagne were raised in a sparkling tribute to a business transaction, baseball or soccer well played, even an outstanding report card.

Following a salute to the massive Confederate battle flag that dominated the upper half of the south wall, Mr. Abbott Bristol Stonemason, widower and master of his manor, would read poetry, sometimes one of Shakespeare's many sonnets.

As young children, Prudence Grace Ann and her younger brother, Tate, recited poems, not to swagger for attention, but to please Great-Granddad. On many a Christmas Eve, hosts of candles lighted the library into flickering festivity, and following dinner, A.B. produced half-moon eyeglasses, polished them with a dramatic flourish, and read *A Christmas Carol* by Charles Dickens. Tate grew up comparing Ebenezer Scrooge to his crusty and atheistic great-grandfather. A comparison he kept to himself.

One Christmas, when Great-Granddad had a hoarse throat, he asked Vidalia to pinch-hit. She pleasantly surprised the gathering with her own seasonal selection, Truman Capote's *A Christmas Memory*.

"We elderly aunties," she explained to Prudence and Tate, "tend to appreciate one another."

There was also a traditional household party, with all the Stonemasons, plus every domestic member. Gifts to the manor staff were heartily presented by A.B. himself. Never tokens, but sums of substance to reward loyalty to the hearth and heritage. Shares of stock in Stonemason Enterprises.

Tate could not recall a single servant ever resigning, nor one being discharged.

Vidalia ran this household, not in pomposity, but with a reserved altruism, demanding high standards. *Proper* was one of her favorite terms, a word she personified. A few elderly friends called her Viddy; to most of the populace, however, she was addressed as Miz Vidalia, a respected lady who respected others and herself.

Often, almost always, she wore white. In the young mind of Tate Bannock Stonemason, his petite great-aunt made white appear more pure. Perhaps it was her sugar-white hair.

Prior to the aircraft tragedy, Tate had been suspended from school for two days. Miss Easton, who taught English, caught him decorating her blackboard with his creativity:

Is a bear Catholic?
Does the Pope pee in the woods?

As they would riotously support any prank of questionable taste, the class yelped its approval. No one, however, could outbellow their anal-retentive and ulcer-plagued principal, Horace X. Flannigle, a former football coach with the IQ of a Milky Way bar and the temper of Thor. Mercifully, he overruled Miss Easton's hasty suggestion that Tate be electrocuted, and instead sent him packing, not to reappear until Monday.

He was ordered to return to school with a sincere letter of apology to Miss Easton.

17

No one in Tate's family was made aware of this happenstance, with one exception. Compelled to tell somebody, he avoided home and scampered to the manor house. In the brain of the banished, Vidalia might have a forgiving face.

Together, they sat on white wicker chairs in the sunroom, basking in each other's company. Tate told her what had happened. After a guarded smile, Vidalia straightened her spine and summarized his joke as having more levity than elegance.

"I have to write an apology."

"Don't expect *me* to write it, Mr. Tate. You waltzed, so *you* pay the orchestra." Vidalia wiped amusement from her eyes. "Does our fragile Miss Easton have a sense of humor?"

"Slightly more than a parking meter."

"Are you sorry? If so, Mr. Tate, at least you could try to appear contrite in her presence."

"I'm sorry the world's become so serious. Almost every day in *The Orlando Sentinel* there's a whiner who's ticked off by some little wisp of trivia." Looking at Vidalia, he asked, "Have *you* ever been offended by anything?"

She thought for a moment. "Not severely, child. Only weaklings are offended. We who are strong are more profitably occupied. Offense rolls off me like rain off a roof."

He'd sat there, adoring the woman who smiled so sweetly at him, eyes revealing her inner shine.

"I wonder," Tate asked her, "have Americans lost their ability to laugh? Yesterday, at school, a girl told a joke and some guys chuckled. But then, a group of nerds accused them of . . . incorrect laughter."

"What's the joke?"

"You might not get it."

Eyebrows arching, her chin rising an inch, Vidalia informed him. "The term *might not* also implies the converse, allowing for the possibility that I *could*, as you say, *get it*."

Tate grinned. "Okay, here goes. A chef is writing a new cookbook on French food, and titles it . . . *Let Them Eat Marie Antoinette*."

"Please don't explain it."

"There's a whole series of these punch lines making the rounds, online. For example, a cookbook for aliens, called *Let Them Eat Sigourney*. Or a cannibal cookbook, *One Foot in the Gravy*."

"Any other observations?"

"Well," he said, "getting back to how starchy our society's become, when a buddy of mine wrote a piece on childhood games for our school newspaper, he'd listed Cowboys and Indians. The paper's faculty adviser, Mr. Cramps, whose funny bone was shot off in a hunting accident, changed the name of the game to, get this, Cowpersons and Native Americans."

"Politically correct," said Vidalia with a sigh, "is too repressive for me. It's absurdity." She paused to reflect. "Mr. Tate, all of our delightful drivel isn't drafting your letter. So let's focus on target."

Getting up, Vidalia had walked sedately into A.B.'s study. She returned with a yellow legal pad, pencils, and a pair of books on etiquette by Amy Vanderbilt and Letitia Baldrige.

19

"This one's newer," she said, checking an index, then reading what Miss Baldrige advised. "If possible, one should apologize verbally, right on the spot. Then hand-deliver a personal note. And consider flowers."

Tate sighed. "How do I begin?"

"Start your letter with manners, Mr. Tate, a virtue that Miss Easton may doubt that you possess. Establish that chivalry is not beyond you. What does she like? At the moment we can most assuredly rule out *you*."

"She likes good lit. If she reads a particular passage from a book she's touting, sometimes she cries. A few kids smirk, but to me, it's sort of a beautiful cool. Miss Easton probably doesn't suspect that, in a way, I sort of admire her."

"Then tell her so, Mr. Tate." She raised a warning finger. "Be genuine. Try to remember a phrase she read that truly touched you and express your appreciation. Miss Easton may believe in good faith that the two of you fervently share something fine. And thereby see fineness in you."

He had smiled at her then, and kissed her cheek, on that afternoon in the manor's sunroom. She had returned his warmth.

"Aunt Vidalia, how did you become so clever?"

She had thought for a moment, then answered.

"Surviving."

THE TORTURE IN HIS LEG INTENSIFIED.

Oliver drove Tate to Callahoochee Regional for a checkup, to the hospital's new wing, which housed a physiotherapy clinic. Earlier, both his great-grandfather and Vidalia had offered to go with him, yet Tate had insisted on going alone.

Holding the open door of the resplendent gray Bentley, their uniformed driver seemed to force a brave smile. "I hope those medical people give you good news, Mr. Tate. Truly do. I be close by, and I'll bring the car to the front door soon's I spot you departing."

"Thank you, Oliver." Tate paused. "All of you, the entire staff at the manor, have been continually considerate. At times, I've been in a gloomy funk. Maybe even grumpy. Y'all know our family took quite a blow. We do appreciate your concern, and we're most grateful."

"A dreadful shame, Mr. Tate, losing Miss Prudence, who'd

blowed me a good-bye kiss." Oliver hung his head, then looked up. "But nobody stronger than my Mr. Abbott. And also Miz Vidalia. In all my years at the manor house, I never know a flimsy Stonemason."

"Nor have I. I'll try to be out soon, Oliver, and thank you for waiting for me."

The reception room smelled fresh, yet with a hospital's hint of scrubbed sterility. A long coffee table held a number of rumpled magazines, including a month-old issue of *Sports Illustrated*. After a jolting hesitation, Tate selected it, as well as a chair. On the front cover was a color photograph of a baseball player, a pitcher whose name he had known quite well for several seasons. This man had been his ideal. Boonell Bunkum. He was both cover and cover story, one featuring a bold thick-lettered headline to catch a reader's eye:

BOO SIGNS FOR $30,000,000

Deep in the shadowy reaches of his mind, a voice seemed to be whispering to him in a taunting tone: "Tater Stonemason and the Atlanta Braves finally agreed, his agent announced earlier today. The young pitching sensation flew to Atlanta to ink a seven-year contract for the incredible sum of . . . of . . . providing, of course, that the rookie's leg . . ."

A nurse in white appeared.

Tate was guided down a corridor and into a therapeutic facility. A test. One more test, as though he hadn't already been X-rayed, poked, and prodded in full. But his brain

22

tuned out. The hypothetical sportscaster kept linking his name to the Braves.

"Go right in, Mr. Stonemason."

"Thank you."

Why were so many white-coated lab technicians X-raying his leg again?

"Hold still." ZAP.

"Don't move now." ZAP. ZAP.

They needed more X rays of his femur, tibia, and fibula, shots of the pin inserted in his acetabulum. White coats discussed his shattered ankle bones, attempting to bend his right leg until his knee wailed into near insanity. As usual, they punctured his flesh with needles.

"Does this hurt? Could you feel that? Try and tell us exactly what you're experiencing."

Lying on the hard table, Tate couldn't inform them of how five of the dearest people in his life were snatched away and roasted by flame. His sister, Prudy, a high-school valedictorian and soccer cocaptain, accepted at Auburn, Emory, Tulane, and Flagler, would never get to go. Their parents, Charles Boyd Stonemason and the former Amelia Booth Bannock, both dead. Also his grandparents, Judge Jackson Royster Stonemason and his wife, who had been Dolly Madison Tate.

Vulcanized and vanished.

So beyond feeling mere needles, he'd become impervious to bayonets.

"Severe myositis. The muscle is still inflamed, plus there's anterior tibial disorder. Permanent nerve damage, I'm afraid,

23

which leads to muscular atrophy. The lower limb's nerves are so traumatized that recovery is remote. . . ."

The kaleidoscope of voices faded.

Nothing new. Never would he run or walk normally without hesitation or a crutch. Intense pain, unless he constantly maintained a prescribed analgesic level in his bloodstream. Tate had taken morphine, codeine, and endless bottles of aspirin until he could barely digest food and his ears were ringing.

"Sciatic nerve damage, a lot more than minor. Say, aren't you the young fellow who played baseball at . . ."

Someone must have nudged the speaker, but the hushing came a bit late. About six months late, going on seven.

"Sorry," a sheepish voice repented.

"It's all right," Tate said, to ease the fellow's embarrassment. "Only weaklings are offended, and I don't intend to remain weak." He faked a laugh. "Besides, our entire team was super, and we're grateful y'all rooted for us."

The room became silent except for a distant hum of electronic medical gadgets, mindlessly working their technical wonders beyond a layman's comprehension. Eyes closed, Tate breathed the familiar smell, one he'd recently escaped, yet it kept recapturing his nostrils and returning them in handcuffs.

Hands helped him from the table.

"Thank you. I can walk by myself." Then he fell, and they hesitated to assist. Untouched, he reeled toward the exit door. "Watch me," he said over his shoulder. "Hold me on, because I'm fixing to steal second."

With a hand sometimes steadying himself on the wall, he managed to walk alone down the long corridor, heading toward where reliable old Oliver would be waiting nearby. Passing through Reception, a familiar voice pleasantly called his name.

"Tater?"

Before seeing her, he knew. Angelina!

Since the disaster, Tate had seen absolutely no one from his high school. A few baseball buddies had hung around the hospital but were not allowed to visit his room. Family only. And, he presumed, no one knew that he now lived with his great-grandfather and great-aunt Vidalia at Stonemason Manor.

Sooner or later, however, he accepted that someone would crack the ice. Open his cage. Perhaps it was fate that Angelina Della-Rialto had been, on this day, chosen.

They had taken classes together; not many, yet enough to exchange smiles. A few words. Several times she had caught him looking at her and seemed to be pleased. Nothing more. Strange: Only a day or two before the plane crash, Tate had decided to ask her to a dance. Angie Della-Rialto attracted him.

A pretty girl. Brains, manners.

A minister's daughter.

"Hi," he said.

Not much of a greeting. One that sounded pathetically lame. Well, if anyone could personify lameness, it was he.

"Welcome back, Tate. I'm not following you. Honestly. I was here for a flu shot, fixing to leave, when I spotted you

25

being led along the hall. Forgive me, but I was compelled to wait. To say hello."

"Thanks. I'm . . . I'm glad you did."

"Really?"

Tate nodded.

"We miss you at school. What happened to you, and to your family, sort of neutralized everyone's sense of humor." She looked at the floor. "I'm not saying all of this too smoothly."

"You're saying it just fine."

"Your sister Prudy was some gal." She paused. "There are no words, you know. None. All I can do is this." She touched his hand.

The gesture made him flinch.

How could she understand his destroyed leg? He was nothing now, except a confused collection of scars and burns. Part of an ear missing. Tracks of countless stitches. Her touch was probably pity for a freak.

"Excuse me, please. Oliver's waiting for me, and I'd better be going home. And thank you."

As he started toward the hospital's front door, he lost control of his leg. Tate would have fallen again had she not caught him. Surprising how strong soccer girls are.

"You shouldn't have to do this, Angelina."

"Hey! It's what friends are for."

ASH.

In his hands, the resplendence of blond wood was gleaming with a muted yellow hue, not unlike the near-white outer petals of a dandelion.

Perched on the edge of his bed, Tate gripped thirty-four inches of vibrantly lathed lumber, a sculpted silo of a barrel that gradually tapered down to a pine-tar handle, with a customary knob at the heel. A sturdy sword for demolishing a slider. What a ballbreaker! He preferred ash to metal.

"How odd I am," he was telling the bat. "Talk about a split personality, that's Tater, the diamond dichotomy. Half hitter and half pitcher."

How true.

At the plate he had been a get-on-base batsman who'd often set the table for the upcoming top of the order. Not burly enough to crack homers, but a line-drive hitter with the aggressive speed to stretch a single for two. He'd bide his time at the plate, making the opposing pitcher sweat, whenever possible working him into a full count, fouling off marginal pitches to tire the guy's arm. As a pitcher himself, he knew what pitchers hated, so rarely did he swing at a first pitch. The mounders he faced were all savvy enough to heed his batting average, which hovered over three hundred.

Thus, to him, first pitches were not frequently fat, because this hurler wasn't a pussy out.

Eight seasons ago, when he'd first entered Little League, it had been Vidalia, his great-aunt, who had taught him bats-manship, as she had also coached his father. And before that, his grandfather, as they had grown up together. Even though Vidalia was ten years older.

Tate could still hear her wise instruction: "Watch the ball, sugar. Keep your bat back and begin to swing on every pitch, but don't follow through until it looks tasty. Take your cut at the ball's top half, slightly north of its equator."

"Why?" he had asked her. "Why the top half?"

"On account of a pop-up is a snap to catch. But a grounder, well-stroked, is a line drive that bounces. An infielder has to move in front of it, judge a good hop, field it, throw. And then the firstsacker has to catch the peg with his cleats on the bag. A lot of variables. That's why."

As he sat on the luxurious bed in one of the elegant antique-furnished bedrooms, now his room, Tate was remembering when he was only eight, and how he had always addressed his first coach.

"Aunt Vidalia, how come you know so much baseball?

You said you've never *played* it, not even once."

"Well," she had answered, "now that you're growing too hefty to cuddle on my lap as we used to, I will whisper you a secret. My very first toy was a baseball. I didn't have a mother or a father, but I was one fortunate little girl."

"Why were you fortunate?"

"In place of parents, I had me a whole baseball team!"

"Honest?"

She crossed her heart.

"We were called Ethiopia's Clowns."

"Were you living here with Great-Granddad?"

"Not until I turned ten. Before that, my home wasn't a house at all." She leaned closer to him. "It was an old purple bus. And my folks were all black baseballers."

"Aunt Vidalia, are you spoofing me?"

"No, sweet pea, not a mite. Sometime, when you are mature enough to listen up to the entire story, I'll fill your little ears with the ballads of baseball." One by each, she touched his freckles with a fingertip. "Enough of yesterday. Right now, as you hit, keep your little right elbow up. Higher! It'll help to level out your swing, so you cut *through* the ball, not *at* it. A level swing is possibly what made Ted Williams the most picturesque of all batsmen."

Recalling those treasurable times, when his family had been whole, Tate clenched the bat handle, fingers tightening until his knuckles whitened. Why? Why couldn't he now close his eyes and retreat into early boyhood, a carefree age eight, when his great-aunt had given him his first bat?

Vidalia also hand-made his first baseball.

He still had it, formed over a golf ball so it would be small, white leather, one endless curving seam that Vidalia had stitched by needle. A fit for little fingers.

"Day by day," Tate reminisced aloud, "you drilled my throwing, and how to grip a curve, and that a knuckler didn't involve knuckles, only fingernails." He laughed. "I still can't control it."

At his early Little League outings, Vidalia's discerning eye recorded details. Game after game, she took copious notes, explaining, for example, why only a foolish runner at third base takes a lead on the chalk line. There, if hit by a batted ball in fair territory, he's out. Instead, he should back up a foot or two, to leave the base on foul ground.

Vidalia stressed pitching.

"A smart hurler," she said one afternoon as she gripped a baseball, "needs only two talents. Speed and location. A pitcher who attempts too much finger flick, or spit, is a fool. The best *stuff* he puts on a ball is control."

"Any other secrets?"

"Throw strikes. Especially with an itchy runner on first, eyeing second. Usually the hitter's patient, to allow the runner to size up a pitcher's moves. If the batter waits two throws, both strikes, he's in a hole. Meaning he must protect the plate from your next pitch, which breaks away."

"How can I remember all that?"

"You won't have to, cotton babe. Just remember two weapons, heat and strike-zone location." Bending close to his ear, she whispered, "Vary each one."

"What exactly does *heat* mean?"

"Speed."

Years passed. Aunt Vidalia crafted him toward becoming the complete and sophisticated player. At the time, Tate was too young to understand why she was bothering. He asked. She told him.

"You, celestial one, are my final Stonemason baseball prodigy, the star I want to launch and propel into Cooperstown. You're it, Mr. Tate. My bottom of the ninth, down a run, with two out and a full count."

"It's *that* important?"

"To me, very. Someday I'll share with you my reason. But the Hall of Fame is many strikes, games, and seasons from today. Now then, I have reached a conclusion about your abilities, regarding their limitations. You're not going to be a slugger."

"No, I'm too lean and lanky to swat bleacher balls. All I'll do is fly long outs."

"Exactly. But with you as a hot-hitting pitcher, the National League will be more than mildly interested. Would you like to master a mound?"

Tate had nodded.

"Very well." With a long length of measured clothesline, Vidalia established a definite distance. "Sixty feet," she announced, "and six inches."

"Pitcher's rubber to home."

"On the nose."

"Now what?"

Vidalia winked. "For starters, we shall isolate what I call the disputed territory, the most contested and consecrated piece of property in America. Home Plate, U.S.A. Seventeen white rubbery inches, slightly gritty, yet hallowed ground."

"I already know all this stuff."

"Allow my continuing, Mr. Tate, if you please." With a hand on his shoulder, she had pointed to the place that was sixty feet distant. "Here we are on the mound, in altitude a few inches higher than the plate."

"What are you telling me?"

"You, the pitcher, own the mound. And over there, the batter commands his batter's box. Ah! Who owns home? Your folks know real estate because they so often buy it and sell it for a proceed." Vidalia held up a finger. "But an American youngster's first big real-estate deal is merely seventeen inches wide. Home plate. Two players are about to fight for the fiefdom. Transfer of title. Ownership. Regarding land, it's called fee simple absolute. Who are those two people?"

"Pitcher and batter."

"Right. Now let's use our imaginations." She'd pointed. "See? Observe what the hitter's doing, leaning into and over the plate, to claim it. As a right-handed batsman, he's aware that your right-handed curve will break down and away. So he leans an inch into the strike zone. Are you, as a pitcher, going to let him usurp what ought to be your domain?"

"No. But how do I prevent that?"

"There are ways." Vidalia's mouth made a gentle smile. "One way is to whistle him a little chin music."

"Throw at his head?"

Vidalia's grin widened. "Well, a batter calls it a *beaner*, while a pitcher merely shrugs off such a pitch as a *brush back*. A warning! If a hitter tries to claim the plate's turf, a pitcher is expected to breeze a fastball high and tight, Nolan Ryan style, to caution him that the plate isn't his."

"Whose is it?"

"It's negotiable. Up for grabs."

"I really like the way you explain a thing. Our Little League coaches never did this. They weren't real coaches, of course. Just dads. My dad coached Little League for one season, and that was all. He told me that the kids were super, but the parents drove him crazy." He looked at Vidalia. "Do mothers and fathers understand what you just explained to me about the plate's being up for grabs?"

"Some do. I pity people who don't know baseball, because the game is a part of being an American. It's the fabric of our flag. On a Sunday afternoon in a small town, an insignificant ball game brings folks together a lot more than any single church."

"*You* go to church, Aunt Vidalia."

"I do," she said softly. "Sunday morning belongs to my most precious Lord." She tossed the baseball up about a foot and caught it. "But a summery Sunday afternoon I hold in my hand."

Tate stared up at Vidalia for a moment without speaking. Then he said, "I surely am certain why Great-Granddad and my great-grandmother Lavinia adopted you." He grinned. "And that you kind of adopted *me*."

They had stood for a few seconds, both of them holding a baseball. One hand was black; the other, which was a bit

33

smaller, white. How easily their fingers entwined.

Tate had nodded. "You're right," he told her. "It truly *is* a part of Sunday, but it's also a little bit like church."

They gave each other a hug.

Now, years later, on the brink of seventeen, Tate Bannock Stonemason was no longer dreaming of Cooperstown and the Hall of Fame. He was envying someone he had never met in person, a pitcher in the majors named Boonell Bunkum.

"Wow!"

In a sudden rush of emotion, all that Vidalia had taught him about baseball ebbed into vapor. Bewilderment fogged his mind, now in a confusion of fact and fantasy, whetted by an adolescent greed for glory.

"I could have been a star."

Glancing to his left, he noticed his collection of athletic trophies, a row of cheap Olympian statues presented to him, as well as to all his teammates, over the years. Little League litter. At the time, he had treasured each trophy, and Vidalia had beamed with pride. Now they seemed little more than the fruit of frivolity.

Useless as his right leg.

Before he could govern his temper, the baseball bat he had been holding was cocked. Then, swing upon swing, Tate devastated the sour souvenirs of yesterday, bashing them to shards and splinters.

Each honor pulverized into rubble.

Book II

VIDALIA

5

AN ODIOUS NOISE AWAKENED HER.

For a moment or two, eyes opening, Vidalia Stonemason
continued to lie in her huge four-poster bed, wondering if the
clamor was real or merely a dream. Rising, her feet seeking
and finding bedside slippers, Vidalia was aware that the
cacophony had ceased, replaced by a second sound.

Ballerina barked. Only twice.

Pulling on a white terry-cloth robe, she opened her bedroom door and was immediately met by a coonhound that
no longer barked but softly whined.

"My, my, now show Viddy what's wrong."

Their upstairs hall was dark except for a few small and
strategically placed night-lights. The great downstairs foyer
clock chimed the sixteen-note hour, then bonged once for
one o'clock. As Vidalia slowly scuffed along on the hall's
hardwood floor, she could hear the undisturbed snoring of

Mr. Abbott. As her father was a sound sleeper and slightly deaf, a war wouldn't wake him.

Half asleep, not quite knowing her next move, Vidalia was directed by Ballerina. The dog hobbled to Tate's bedroom and stopped, her nose pressing to one of the panels of curving oak.

"Mr. Tate?" She gently knocked. "Are you all right?"

When he opened the door, bedroom lights blinded her until she could read disturbance on a young face. Although barefooted, Tate was decently covered by faded jeans and a white T-shirt. Beneath its neckline were words:

In case of vertical burial,
THIS END UP

"Hi." Opening the door a bit wider, he whispered, "Come on in. I was rearranging my room and apologize to both you and Ballerina if I woke you."

Entering, she saw broken bits of shiny metal scattered on the Georgia red-oak floor. Vidalia squinted in confusion until she noticed the shelf that usually displayed his athletic trophies.

It was bare and broken.

After Tate had staggered toward his bed, turned, then sat, Vidalia placed her hand on his forehead, feeling the clammy warmth of a fever. Or disposition.

"I'll clean up the mess," he said.

Standing closer to him, she cradled his burning face and head to rest beneath her chin, rocking him with a gentle motion. "There, there, there, Mr. Tate. There's no mess except the trouble that's in your head." Hard to believe, this boy who never cried was sobbing so softly with a hurting that Vidalia would give her life to heal.

"It's night, child. And we have all been struggling up a rocky hill, pulling a wagon of weight. Sometimes, when we fall ourselves down, we sink to the bottom before we can bounce up."

"Oh . . . oh . . . Auntie Vid."

"My stars! Been a pocketful of dreams since you called me that. I recall the time you were three, wee tiny, and somehow rolled around in the potato patch. There you be, smudged all over with dirt. And right then I called you a special name for the very first time."

"Tater."

She kissed his sweaty hair, and to her it tasted like nectar. "That's right," she told him, "because in our world of baseball, a tater is a *home run*!" Still swaying an inch or so from side to side, narrowing her eyes, again trying to breathe his little-boy smell, she said, "My sweet Tater."

Ballerina whimpered.

"Now hush," Vidalia pretended to scold her. "Don't you fret. Mr. Tate is going through a nighttime of fright and fear." Glancing down at the dog who rested one paw on the bedspread, she added, "Mr. Tate believes that's there's only darksome, but all he has to do is wait patient for a dawn. No storm endures forever. There always comes a sunup. Perhaps not the perfect day, but nevertheless a spanking-fresh one."

Resting her chin on Tate's knee, the hound looked up

briefly with questioning eyes, then heaved out an almost silent sigh.

"I'm . . . I'm sorry," Tate said.

"Pay no mind." Vidalia enjoyed her smile that no one else could see, mindful that her manner of speech had regressed to the time when she herself was a child. Long time ago. Yet Vidalia could remember her little-girlhood, the candied experiences. "The sour times," she said, "got throwed off that bus, and we left 'em to lie lonesome in the dust."

Lifting his chin, Tate looked up at her. "What bus?" he asked her. "Is it a bus that you told me about, years ago, when you were coaching me in the backyard?"

"Sure enough be."

Her arms released his head so that Tate could sit tall on the bed. Filling his lungs, he let out a long breath of pent-up air.

"Bad day at the hospital?" she asked.

"No worse than any other. Just routine. Nothing to celebrate." Mouth open, he paused for a second as though there was something more he wanted to tell her, but decided to keep it to himself.

"Let it out," she whispered. "Be free."

He stared at her.

"Vidalia, you are so wise, it's eerie."

"Because I know my child. Never been a mother. Oh, a number of years ago, I ached to be one, to bear my own little bundle of a baby boy and teach him baseball." Vidalia shook her head. "Goodness me. Talk about holding matters in. Deep inside, that's where I've stifled that particular yearning. Until now, I haven't ever mentioned it to anyone or hinted that it was still festering." She felt a bit lightheaded, yet resisted an admission that, as of late, she hadn't been keeping too chipper.

"Are you tired, Aunt Vidalia? You seem somewhat unsteady. Perhaps you ought to return to bed. Come along. I'll walk with you to your room, providing you don't scamper too fast for me."

Her hands held his face.

"Thank you, Mr. Tate. It's pleasing to admire so much Stonemason in you. Kindness, and concern." She shook her head. "After all this night's het-up excitement, sleeping, for me, is plumb out of range."

"Same for me. I'm wired."

Taking the bat from his hand, standing it in its customary corner nook, she said, "Perhaps our time is come."

He stood. "Time for what?"

"Well, you'll soon learn. Let's see if we can creep quietly downstairs, brew a pot of that Constant Comment tea, sit ourselves cozy in rocking chairs out on the south veranda, and swap a few bodacious lies."

"Sounds good."

Ballerina, honoring the late hour, decided not to come along. Instead, she unevenly walked to her customary post outside Vidalia's bedroom door, groaned down, and placed her head on her paws.

They tiptoed into the kitchen.

"Shush," Vidalia warned him, a grin to her lips, "so's we don't awaken Cook. Sometimes that big Zulu gal got a

41

ornery that's hotter than her stove."

Tate frowned. "You're talking a bit strange."

"On purpose." Vidalia had to laugh. "I believe, backstage, it's called Method Acting, priming oneself into character prior to making an entrance." She pointed. "Please hand me that yellow buttercup tray. It's perfect for serving tea."

He smiled her way. "Vidalia, is there anything you don't know? Honestly, is there?"

"Oh, there's a plenty. Because I'm just a plain ol' southern lady, a little lace, lavender, and lilac. Nothing more. And not fancy." She looked softly at him. "Toss me that pink potholder."

In fun, he tossed a green one.

"Limit," she called him.

The tray was finally ready.

"What'll I carry?"

"Carry yourself tall. Even if it's the middle of night, I prefer to take tea in the company of a proper gentleman. So strut your raising."

Outside, a choir of nocturnal bugs had tuned up and were serenading their mates. From a flowered Oriental teapot, Vidalia poured steamy Constant Comment into a pair of bone-china cups on saucers, then passed wedges of lemon.

The initial sip convinced her of how awake she was, despite the wee hours, and also how idiosyncratic this might promise to be, to her, to both of them. For over half a century, Vidalia had resisted endowing her past to anyone, not even to family. Like vintage wine, she had bottled and corked her life into a cellar of black obscurity. Yet tonight was the occasion to share its bounty.

For innermost reasons and longings, a majority of them too intrinsic to divulge, Vidalia aspired to have this story told, to her beloved Tater, eventually to all of America.

Not for herself. But for Ethiopia's Clowns.

6

"PLAY BALL!"

Little Viddy's earliest memories included sitting in the merciless heat of a visitors' dugout. Across the field, the home-team players always sat in a shelter with its backside to the sun, providing shade. She was merely a black speck of life, wedged on a hard plank bench between her two gods.

Wash and Cappy.

She had learned to walk and to talk, but because so many fans were shouting, cheering, razzing, there wasn't much chance to git heard. So Viddy quietly perched, swinging her bare legs and feet forward and back, sometimes just staring down at her dirty toes and wondering what it would actual be like to own shoes.

Out yonder, on the dirt and dandelion places, a home team had taken the field. Nine white strangers. Mr. George Washington, the pitcher who sat beside her, had taught her how to count up to nine. Yesterday, in a different town, Wash convinced her that *nine* was the most important number in baseball. For three reasons: nine defensive positions, nine innings, and nine was the number on his back.

"Ten," Wash insisted, "is only for bowling."

Their team, called Ethiopia's Clowns, was always, always, always up to bat first. Why? Cappy, whose given name was Ethiopia, had explained.

"Sweetness, we'll never bat last on account that's what home teams do, and us Clowns don't got a home. All we own is each other and a purple bus." Cappy had give her a warm hug with a tickle inside it. "But instead of every single home, or homer, in the U.S. of A., I druther have *you*."

She eventual learned that Cappy and Wash served as their battery: the catcher and pitcher.

Cappy got called such because he was, by rights, Mr. Ethiopia Jones, the eldest, and the official team captain. If he got tanked, Cappy either dried to sober or bailed out of jail. Whenever his breath smelled worse than a slaughterhouse sewer pipe, Cappy'd whine, push her away, and say, "Sorry, kid . . . this ol' spade is hung."

Wash didn't drink at all.

Perhaps he'd taken a nip or two years ago, before the Epiphany Tent Revival Soul Saviours happened to arrive at a ballpark, a bit early for some Sunday evening evincement, before the ball game (which happened to stretch into extra innings) had ended.

They'd all seen revivals before. This one, however, wasn't white people. All of the Epiphany Saviours were blacker than

45

Ethiopia, including their spellbinder, Sister Glorify, who happened to attract Wash's bloodshot eye. At the time, Wash Washington had only one eye working, as the other had been swellingly closed in a fight with Junebug. It was over the rights to flirt up Sister Glorify, a name that rhymed with horrify, according to Cappy.

Junebug—their shortstop—and Wash had physically disagreed once before because of another lady, several towns ago, named Flam. Her middle name was Mable. Together she was Flam-Mable. Viddy guessed it somehow related to *heat*, which, Wash spelled out, was throwing a fastball.

After they'd made three outs, Ethiopia's Clowns took the field, all in their rumpled gray uniforms trimmed with purple (hence the color of their bus) and canary yellow. It hadn't taken Viddy long to master all of their names. The outfielders: Catfish, Swizzlestick, and Dawg. In the infield, third around the horn to first: Hookworm, Junebug, Nap, and Tonic.

The first baseman earned the nickname because whenever he spotted a pretty lady in the crowd, what he called one of Feline Africana, ol' Tonic would duck into the bus and douse his hair with a concoction that, according to Cappy, could either kill weeds or poison rats. During a lull in the game (often caused by a friendly fracas, which, in a town called Fayette, broke out in the bandstand between a drummer and a clarinetist), Tonic sometimes eased himself into the bleachers, to allow the lady to apply her nostrils to his hair.

Choice seating was behind home plate, beyond a stretch of chicken wire dented by foul balls, and beneath a leaky roof.

During the change of half innings, Cappy rehearsed Viddy on how to read. A book was unnecessary because a wooden fence beyond the outfields featured a galore of billboards, each with a package, lettering, and a few termites. In no time at all Viddy could recite inspirational verses for products such as: Mail Pouch Tobacco, Gilman's Grits, Burma-Shave, Calumet Baking Powder, Bull Durham, Tube Rose Snuff, and the Morton Salt umbrella girl's promise, "When it rains, it pours."

"We got only one rule," Cappy explained to Viddy. "Whatever else we do, we dasn't win. But we play so much smoother than all these yokels, it's fun to worry 'em sick."

"Cappy's right," Wash put in. "Most teams we go against are nothing but weekend warriors, while us Clowns play almost ever day."

A fact Wash Washington omitted was that the Clowns rode a bus all night, arguing as to whose turn at driving it was, and practicing their favorite midnight hobby: getting lost.

"Cappy," she asked in the dugout, "how soon's I going to drive the bus?"

"Not until you five."

"I be six. Or seven."

"Seven? Gosh, where the summer gone?" Then he smiled at her and sang a morsel of song: "Oh, it ain't necessarily so . . ."

This game, like all the others, breezed right along. Cappy believed in short games. No extra innings. The Clowns allowed a bunch of runs in the ninth, just enough to keep the local fans from burning their purple bus. The trick wasn't to win. The whole secret was to play the game close, with disguised and deliberate errors. Clowns would hit a ball and then leg it for third instead of first. With runners on third and second, they'd pull a reverse steal, breaking back to second and first.

Stealing home from first base always brought laughter from the crowd. It was an unexpected prank.

"Watch this, honeypot," Wash had earlier been telling Viddy. "Before we start, our boys are going to play a ghost game. That means without any ball."

The Clowns' pitcher pretended to pitch the nonexistent ball, and Nap, as substitute catcher, pretended to catch it and throw it back. Junebug, bat in hand, swung at the invisible ball, then hustled for first, as two outfielders ran to snare a ball that wasn't there and collided.

"The crowd eats it up," Wash said.

When regular play had resumed, the Clowns put a runner on first, Swizzlestick, as Catfish came to the plate and popped up a high bunt. Breaking for second, Swiz veered, galloped up behind the mound, pointed up at the ball, and hollered, "I got it." For some reason, the infielders all froze in surprise as the ball hit dirt. Cat scooted easy to first while Swiz was already resting on second.

Even the home-team rooters slapped their legs as if to indicate a lenient approval.

Following inning number nine, the white manager of the local winners ambled over to the Clown dugout to shake hands with Cappy.

"Ethiopia Jones, by the jingle, it's a bona fide enjoyment having y'all back here to town. Better'n breakfast."

Cappy grinned, then shook his head. "We can't seem to outdo you fellers. You do too much baseball for us poor simpers."

The manager gave Cappy's shoulder a friendly punch. "Like fun. You rascals can play circles around our boys, and both of us know it. Ya got a dandy right fielder. What's his name?"

"Dawg. A fifteen-year-old runaway. His mama's boyfriend beat up on him fearful, and worse, *she* stood watching." Cappy frowned. "Never knowed his real daddy. Come to think about it, neither did I ever learnt mine."

"That's sorry. But he's a player, Cap. That boy's so fleet that I bet he could steal Ty Cobb's underwear. He's another Cool Papa."

Cappy said, "Thanks. But white or black, ain't ever going to be a base runner faster than Cool."

The white manager pointed down at Viddy. "What ya got there, Cap? Where'd you find this little black pearl?"

With his one hand, Cappy pulled Viddy closer to his side. "Years back, somebody do a dumb stunt and leave her in our team bus. We finded a baby under a seat. Shoddy thing to do. But we was already miles and miles out of town, so we kepted her." Smiling down, he touched Viddy's face. "She my baby. Raise her on goat's milk whenever we could locate it. When we couldn't, on beer."

"No bigger than a skink."

"Not much. Dawg and Vidalia be close friends, maybe on

49

account both be children. Dawg's teached her how to chuck. She may be skinky small, but my Vidalia's a mighty mite. Oughta see her throw." Cap handed her a baseball. "Honeypot, show our nice Mr. Cameron how to peg."

Winding up, Viddy threw it a rod.

"Say," the gentleman said in a surprised voice. "That little kid's got a wing."

"More'n that," Cappy told him. "My precious here can *read*. Quicker than anybody on the Clowns, including Wash."

Mr. Cameron knelt to look straight into her eyes and smiled friendly. "A perty miss, you be. A fine child." Looking up at Cappy, he asked, "Did you honest name her Vidalia?"

"Sweetest onion ever was. Them special Vidalia grow right out of the heart of Georgia, where I hailed from. And they're even a lick sweeter than a Georgia peach."

"Sweeter than Cobb?"

Both men tossed back their heads to holler up a hoot, the kind of laughter that holds its sides.

Once again, Cappy's brawny arm nestled her nearer to him, and his smile shone down at her like a summer sun. "Oh," he sang to her, "I jus' wild about Viddy. And she jus' wild about me."

Mr. Cameron laughed.

Cappy looked at him. "Say, I don't suppose there be any chance that us visiting ballplayers might git allowed to partake a sit-down supper in that spanky new restaurant in town?"

Viddy noticed the good nature drain from Mr. Cameron's

white face, as he couldn't seem to look Cappy in the eye. Instead, he just examined his dusty tan shoes. "Don't guess I know how to answer you." As he rested an easy hand on Cappy's sweaty-wet shoulder, his voice faded off like he was ashamed of his words. "I don't know how to answer you straight out."

Cappy sighed. "You already done."

7

THE BUS ROLLED AND RATTLED THROUGH THE NIGHT.

But at four o'clock and still pitch-dark, they hit it lucky. Wash somehow spotted a bakery that started heating up at early morn and bought six bags of jelly doughnuts, cupcakes, and three pies. Later on, to rinse it all down, where they stopped to trade for gasoline, Cappy located an entire case of warm Coca-Cola.

"Viddy," said Dawg, "you got powdery sugar all over you's mouth, just like a comical ol' mustache." He laughed. "I want one, too."

Sleepily she asked, "Where we at?"

"Child, we ain't exact no place, headed for nowhere, and lost, because Mr. Washington is driving. But by afternoon, sugarbeet, we certain best be at Claxton."

Turned out that Claxton was a heap of happy, because they was celebrating Italian-American Day. Half the town, as Cappy worded it, was of Eye-talian persuasion, brewed grape wine, and worshiped both Mussolini and Mother Cabrini, even though they never got married.

"I got us a idea," Wash proclaimed.

"Trouble," moaned Cappy. "I smell it coming 'round the bend."

"Now hold on," said Wash. "This'n is a sure laugher. In place of our customary names, we'll all claim to be Irish. I'll be Kelly. You can pose as O'Hara. Today, our team is the Irish Terriers, and everybody's a Mickey."

All the Clowns hooted their approval.

"Reckon I'll be Hoolihan."

"Okay, I be Murphy."

"Me, I'll be McShea."

Cappy grinned. "I hafta admit this game be amusement of a idea." He turned to Wash. "Who you fixing to be?"

"McMouse."

Curled close to Cappy's mountain of a chest, Viddy tried to sleep. But the boys all were whooping so loud, it made her wonder what was up.

Wash proved right. At the Claxton ballpark, soon's the plate umpire raised up a megaphone to his mouth, faced the grandstand, and read off Irishy names for an all-colored team, the Italian-American Day people near to laugh silly.

"Ya see," Wash explained his caper to Viddy, "the Claxton Po-lice Department happen to be mostly Irishers, who don't act too lenient at the populace that's Eye-talian. Get it?"

In a fog, Viddy nodded.

"So," said a beaming Wash, "that's how come I brain-farted us Ethiopia's Clowns to assume Irishy names. All in fun, honeypot. Just laughs."

The game against the Claxton Champs didn't turn out so joyous, as the Champs had partook of the *vino* all night, like the Irish Terriers had rode a bus. The yawning crowd appeared ready to ask for their money back, and Cappy scratched his head in worry.

"No," he sang in a sorrowful voice, "it don't mean a thing if it ain't got that swing." To Viddy he said, "Best we spark up this ball game, right now, because the people don't aim to clap, cheer, or even throw a pop bottle at the ump. Our comedy is tragical."

Right then, the worst sounds that Viddy had ever heard arrived: the Sons of Italy Gold Cornet Marching Band, so somebody said. In they paraded, out of step and out of tune, each man playing a different march. They were in uniform, more or less: black hats, white shirts—few of which were tucked into black trousers that were too long—and black work shoes, many untied.

One of the local people yelled. "See their leader, a big guy with a long baton. That's my Uncle Alberto. See him?"

No one could *not* see Uncle Alberto.

He was twice the size of any of the other ungifted musicians who followed him. He wore a bright, satiny sash of red, white, and green; on his chest was an impressive row of medals. A dog walked beside him, tail wagging. Uncle Alberto, a wide smile beneath an even wider mustache, waved to everyone as though he truly knew and loved them all.

"On a day like today," said Cappy, "everbody Italian. Including ever dog in Claxton."

The game was suspended, as playing would be impossible while the Sons of Italy were parading around the bases. One of the Sons dropped a drumstick yet seemed not to care. Baseball fans were now singing, dancing, holding both hands high in the air, and snapping fingers to the bass drum's beat.

"Verdi," someone said. "They're playing Verdi."

"*Si*. And they're losing."

The umpire, at this point, had seen and heard enough Verdi, and perhaps wanted the so-called game to end in order to be paid his three dollars and go home, where it would be quieter. His hands muffled his ears. Although he was a very small man, the umpire summoned the courage to attempt to call the concert to a finish. Walking boldly to where the band would soon be, the little official stopped and waited for the Sons of Italy Gold Cornet Marching Band to round third base (a few actual did trip on it, but only three fell) and head directly toward him.

"Halt!"

Raising a commanding hand, the stern-faced umpire confronted Uncle Alberto, who, knees flexing high, came strutting in his direction, toward home plate. Refusing to yield, the little ump held his ground, looking smaller as the giant drum major drew closer. Uncle Alberto, who continued to smile and parade, bent quickly to scoop the umpire up in his great arms and kissed him.

"That little ol' ump," Wash muttered. "He got a temper

sorrier than a wet cat. Uncle Alberto maybe bitted off more'n he can smooch."

Viddy could easy see that the umpire was still trying to restore order and speak his mind. Yet it wasn't a cinch to maintain dignity when held in the air, carried forward, and kissed by so large a leader with so ticklish a mustache. Uncle Alberto, holding the squirming ump under his chin, continued onward, yet not directly toward home plate. Unsteadily, his monstrous and wayward shoes were trudging toward the pitcher's mound. Once there, he stubbed a toe on the rubber and fell, landing on his unfortunate burden.

"I do," said Wash Washington. "I do so love this curiosity of a town. Makes me wish I was Eye-talian instead of Irish."

One by each, the so-called musicians wheezed Verdi to a hesitant halt; now leaderless, they hurried to the pitcher's mound to raise the *Titanic* off one of her lifeboats. Uncle Alberto didn't seem to be hurt, only crying, and repeatedly crossing himself.

"Alberto!" An appreciative crowd started to chant. "Alberto. Alberto. Viva Alberto!"

Alberto alternately wept and prayed, refusing to stand. His expression became sorrowfully blank, searching, now on hands as well as knees, his massive head turning one way, then another. One of his musicians, a trombonist with a slightly bent slide, yelled over to someone near the Clown (Irish Terrier) dugout.

"Lost one of his medals."

The stands emptied. Fans vacated their seats in order to flood the field with assistance, all eyes examining the sandy turf for a stray decoration. Yet not everyone at the ballpark was combing the ground. The umpire, in a huff, stalked off the field, screaming to anyone willing to listen, "The mayor can keep his cussed three dollars and stick it!"

The ump headed for home.

"I hope *we* git paid," Cappy said, pulling off a sweat-stained baseball cap to scratch his gray woolly hair.

"If'n we don't," Wash remarked with a smirk, "I promise you this here's my final day as a Irish Terrier."

Out on the field, some helpful person seemed to have relocated the misplaced insignia, because the Sons of Italy were attempting another stab at music. Having stabbed poor Mr. Verdi enough, they'd switched over to a waltz. Fans were waltzing, in pairs, except for Uncle Alberto, who was dancing by himself.

Or with the dog.

The game was called because the late afternoon sun was backing off, and a number of patrons, Viddy overheard, had to rush home to milk the goats. Cappy was all smiles; so, Viddy guessed, the team must have pocketed fee money. Thus it was almost a perfect day in Claxton.

After the team had collected their equipment—consisting of eight gloves, a catcher's mitt, shin guards and chest protector, a few balls (mostly used), and their one and only bat—they headed in the direction of the familiar purple bus. Formerly, according to Wash, their vehicle had been used to carry kids to school. Prior to purple, the bus had been painted a bright yellow, some of which could be seen around the fenders, if you looked close at the dents.

Seeing a shiny object, Vidalia bent to retrieve what turned out to be a little lightweight medal. It took some thinking, but Vidalia soon figured what Uncle Alberto lost and cried over. She wanted to keep it, but, by rightful, it wasn't hers to own. A lady bystander was watching them loading the bus, so Vidalia gave the medal to her.

"This is for Uncle Alberto."

The woman looked too awed to answer.

As the bus rolled out of town, Viddy felt proud that she'd returned the medal to its owner. After all, it was probable solid gold. Its letters about shouted importance.

LITTLE ORPHAN ANNIE DECODER PIN

8

Claxton had been a fun place.

But from the moment they pulled into Factoryville, their next stop, Viddy felt a chill. No smiling faces greeted them, only a cold glare of mistrust. The townspeople's eyes were open but empty.

It didn't take Wash Washington long to reason why. This wasn't his first trip to Factoryville; in fact, according to Wash, it was a third visit. So he knew what the place used to be and no longer was. To let the rest of Ethiopia's Clowns in on his discovery, Wash merely nodded his head toward the town's one and only steel mill. "Ain't no smoke coming out of any of those tall chimleys. Usual is. But I suspect the iron-works be quit running."

Shortly after their bus parked outside the closed and pad-locked gate at the ball field, a creamy-colored Cadillac pulled up, spraying cinders, and stopped nearby.

"Here he come." Cappy sucked a discontented tooth. "Fat Jack Antson, the owner of the team, their ballpark, and to hear his bragging, close to everything else."

It took a few grunts, and nearly a crowbar, before Fat Jack could pry hisself from behind the ivory steering wheel and step forward. He had a baby's face.

"Jones," he said to Cappy, without as much as a handshake, "I know the figure I promised ya, boy. Don't expect it. Got tough times hereabouts. So, due to circumstance beyond my control, I gotta chop your cut by better'n a third."

"We gotta eat, Mr. Antson," was all that Cappy said, but not very loud.

"Who don't?"

To Viddy, it was certain plain that Mr. Fat Jack had eaten more than his share of the doughnuts. Bulging over his belt buckle, the man's belly was the size of a beach ball.

Cappy hadn't yet throwed in the towel. "Well, it is sort of a accepted usual, in this baseball business, that a deal's a deal."

"Don't you sass me, boy."

Cappy was twice as old as the Jack person. So how come, Viddy wondered, was Jack calling Cappy a *boy*?

"Take it or leave it," Mr. Antson said, turning his back to Cappy in order to light up a long brown cigar. "I can cancel our game quicker'n squat."

"We'll play. Took us a time to git here, and we fed that bus aplenty gallons of juice."

Mr. Fat Jack smiled without joy. "Now you're becoming smart, boy. You are acting what I call practical." With a chubby hand that sported a diamond pinky ring, Fat Jack flicked an ash from his smoke. "Game's at two o'clock. If we pull in a profitable gate, we'll cut you boys in for a percent, on account I'm known, in my business negotiations, to shoot a stick of straight pool."

Squeezing his overfed body into the Caddy's front seat, he started the engine, then roared off ahead of scattering gravel.

"Wash?"

"Yeah, little doll?"

"Why did that Fat Jack person keep on calling Cappy a *boy*? Cappy be as old as that man's daddy."

Picking her up and holding her close to his heart, Wash explained. "Oh, I don't guess he knows no better. Maybe his dear mama, ol' Missus Fat Jack, never took the time to teach her sonny some proper. Viddy, in spite of his waistline, poor Fat Jack be nothing more'n a small man who thinks he's big. Figures he can stand up tall by hacking down somebody else's legs."

"Do you hate him?" Viddy asked the old pitcher.

"Me? Hate somebody? Sure enough not." Wash looked at her squarely and seemed to be forcing a grin. "Why waste my valuable time disliking somebody bad, when I got a good somebody dear as you to favor?" Holding her in his arms, Wash spun her around in circles, singing, "Oh, sweet and lovely lady be good. Oh, lady be good, to me." Then he stopped.

"Why you crying, Wash?"

"Nah, not me. Never do such. Maybe it be a touch of hay fever." He patted her back with a gentle hand, but his voice

61

turned husky. "I can play by Jack Antson's rules," he seemed to tell the sky, "but it ain't always a snap to explain 'em to our next generation."

At two o'clock Viddy took her position between Wash and Cappy as the Factoryville Foxes, a white team, trotted out on the field. She told Cappy, "Today, I got a mind we shouldn't let Mr. Fat team to win."

Wash and Cappy exchanged glances.

"Ethiopia," said Wash in his snobby voice, "our little Viddy has made us a natty suggestion."

Cap slowly grinned. "Mr. Washington, you convince me." He spat tobacco juice into the dirt and then said, "Hookworm, let's go for a big first inning. Work it however you can."

Next to Swizzlestick, who was leaner than a dry-spell bean, Hookworm Fay was the second-skinniest player. His uniform appeared two sizes too roomy, as if, Wash once remarked, Hook could run three steps before his uniform moved. The poor fit proved profitable. At the plate, Hookworm puffed out his shirtfront, then leaned into an inside curve to let a ball brush cloth.

The ump rewarded Hook with first, a decision that didn't earn local popularity.

Boo-birds hooted a protest.

Up next, Nap laid a bunt to the firstbaser, and, as the pitcher covered the bag, Nap's cleats covered his foot and he dropped the ball.

Two on, and nobody out.

Junebug, hitting third, squared around to bunt, standing

deep in the batter's box, his bat at the catcher's eye level. A muffed knuckler let both runners advance. With first open, Junebug could cut loose.

Their pitcher had other ideas. A high-and-tight caught Junebug's chest letters. Down he went and didn't even twitch.

"Dang," said Cappy, "we only got nine. No sub." Grunting off the dugout bench, he shuffled toward the plate, slow as possible, to allow June a chance to recover. Cap knew all the tricks.

No dice. Junebug just lay moaning.

Nonetheless, the Clown captain helped Junebug to his feet. "We only got nine," he told him.

"I hurt bad, Cappy."

Cap held up his hand. "How many fingers?"

"Three."

"Good." He pointed ninety feet along a freshly chalked straight line. "Now that you can vision, Junebug, what's that little white square down yonder?"

"Uh . . . first base."

With a grin, Cappy said, "Go park on it."

Tonic was fourth in the lineup for good reason. As Wash so often said, "He swing wonderful wood." He did exactly that and hit a triple. Three runs scored.

Back in the dugout, poor Junebug glowered at Cappy, his hand still holding his chest. "You ought to take me out."

"Who do I play at short? Viddy?"

Eyes widening, she asked, "Do I get to play?"

Pinching her cheek in fun, Cappy shook his head.

63

"Honeypot, as the Bums of Bedford Avenue so often say, *wait'll next year*."

"Where," she asked Cappy, "is Bedford Avenue?"

"Brooklyn."

Catfish walked. Dawg was the next Clown hitter, known for his speed in right field and on the paths. But, because he was so young and eager, he was famed for hitting into a double play. Viddy didn't care about that. Dawg was the only one on the team who played little games with her. And he also whispered secrets about Cappy or Wash.

"Viddy," Cappy ordered, "run fast as you can and fetch the long metal file that's in our bus, underneath the driver's seat. And hustle up."

Winded, she returned with the file. Without a word, Cappy lifted a right foot to reside on his left knee and started to file his cleats, changing the angle with every stroke until he produced an ear-piercer of a sound. He grinned and filed faster.

Skreek, scrape, skreek, scrape . . .

"What you up to, Cappy?"

"Oh," he said, "got myself a bit bored, so thought I'd enjoy driving them infielders nuts. They know exact what I be doing, and worrying why, dreading that somebody's going to slash a pivot."

"Pivot?" Viddy had heard that term aplenty of times, thinking the talker was discussing a sore tooth.

"Sugar," said Wash, "if a grounder forces a runner to second, to turn a double play, either the shorty or second baseman has to cover second base, take a quick throw, pivot, and peg to first."

"The middle man?"

Wash pulled her pigtail. "On the nose. Vidalia, never fret that you're stupid. You've got a brain that's sharper than the cleat Cappy's honing up." He pointed. "Look. See that little silver edge smile out of the gritty? Lamb, that there is base running."

Due to their gray hair, and also the fact that the two men were catcher and pitcher, Cappy and Wash hit eighth and ninth in Ethiopia's Clowns batting order. They were stronger on defense than as batsmen, yet today both men hit safely. It was still the top of the first, and the Clowns had batted around, sending the entire nine-man order to the plate.

Errors, in both fielding and throwing to the wrong base, had been made by the Factoryville Foxes, plus their pitcher, in a sweaty suit, had tossed two passed balls that rolled back to the chicken wire, allowing runners to advance. Or score.

As the Clowns' bat (their only) continued to hammer two home-team pitchers, Cappy and Wash scored at a fallout spring. Then, in the dugout, as Viddy was helping to reclip Cappy's purple shin-guards to his trembling legs, a red-faced visitor appeared, who didn't seem pleased by a lopsided score, one that threatened a blowout.

Fat Jack Antson.

"HEY!" HE BELCHED.

Feeling the heat of his voice, Viddy dropped a shin guard and climbed on the bench, near Wash.

"You no-good uppity boys trying to make me a monkey in front of my friends?" He paused to pant. "Y'all ain't getting away with this stunt. Wait'll you see a surprise I got in store."

Without another gasping word, Fat Jack Antson stomped away from the Clowns' dugout, marching to home plate.

"You," he said to the umpire, "whatever the deuce your name is, you're out of here. Fired. So git!"

No sooner had the umpire mumbled something that Viddy couldn't quite hear, when Fat Jack gave him a sudden push in the chest, knocking him to the ground. Before the umpire could regain footing, he was kicked in the sitdown. What dismayed Viddy was that the people watching it all didn't seem to care; they merely stared at the scene as though seeing a blank wall.

To her, their faces were houses with busted windows.

Waving an arm, Mr. Fat Jack summoned a large man to the plate. On the fellow's belt hung two items: a six-shooter revolver in a holster and a thick brown billy club. Then, as Mr. Antson held up both hands, the crowd stilled and waited.

"Folks, this'n here is my cousin from over in Contamitee Falls, where he's a swore-in peace officer. Because our ball game's out of control, we got ourselves a new umpire, Constable Cal Springerman, a man who ain't about to allow dishonesty or poltroony behavior. So this game'll now resume in the right direction."

"In a way," Wash said, "Fat's brung in a ringer."

Cappy agreed. "And it ain't a pretty picture. In this tough old world, there's a lot of different flavors of cop. Good and bad. The one that's standing out yonder, I betcha, is a star with a thug behind it."

"Yup," said Wash, "a bully with a badge."

"Boys," said Cappy, "as my ol' uncle used to claim, most critters in the wild got a sense of realizing when to fight or when to flee."

"Ethiopia," Wash told him, a smirk spreading across his face and showing teeth, "us Clowns best become a *flee* circus."

From that point on, Viddy noticed, it didn't seem to be a ball game. In the field, the Clowns were making on-purpose errors to allow the Factoryvillers to get on base and eventual score. Although it took a spell, the Foxes overtook the Clowns, according to the white numerals on black plates that were now hanging out on the center-field scoreboard. Beneath the two lines of numbers, some words had been neatly printed, which Viddy slowly read:

Hit this scoreboard and win a FREE
box of candy at Klotz's Drugstore.

Nobody came close. The Factoryville Foxes couldn't swat a baseball that distant; and the Clowns, who were in a pickle, had decided to pussyfoot out of town, if allowed, as the losers.

"Ain't much joy," Tonic complained, "when we just got to sweat it out and swallow a beating."

"Sonny boy," Wash told him, "if'n you gander around the park, you'll observe more'n one rowdy holding a axe handle. Or maybe a tire iron. The general mood in this happy hamlet of Factoryville ain't overly merry. Wise up! We's in a one-mill burg and the mill's cold. No paychecks. Kids going to bed hungry. People are people, Tonic. White, black, or pretty pink, out-of-work folks are ripe to rage, to take it out on whoever's handy, usual us out-of-towners."

Tonic spat. "You and Cappy be two of a kind. Old geezers who do nothin' except . . . *tiptoe careful*."

Cappy chimed in. "Young'n, that is precise how me and Mr. Washington here outlasted the odds long enough to become old geezers."

It made Vidalia smile. But then, to make Tonic feel better, she reached out to rub a sore place on his elbow. "You in a misery?" she asked him.

"Yeah, I'm in Factoryville."

"It's my fault," Wash fessed. "I be the roadie who swaddled us into this undoing, so heap a blame on me. In good faith, boys, I didn't know the mill would be closed down and the steelers locked out."

"Hard times," the catcher said.

Wash looked at him. "Ethiopia, nary a soul of us ever saw easy. You and me wouldn't recognize Easy Street if one of its gold bricks jumped out and nipped us on the rump."

"Wash," Viddy asked, "what's a *rump*?"

Draping his arm around her shoulders, the pitcher pointed to the large new umpire, the one wearing a club. "Well," he said, "to edificate you on the subject, for starters, a rump is a backside, and it general exist in two parts. There's one of 'em behind that badge. The other buttock calls itself Mr. Fat Jack."

To Viddy, the ball game seemed to last all day long. Nobody had a good time or razzed the ump. During the bottom of the seventh inning, the Good Lord Above took pity and let loose a thunder-boomer of a rainstorm that filled an inky sky with high-tension wires. When the game got called, the Clowns got paid off with an amount that was a few pennies short of an insult, so they packed up and took to their purple bus.

"Dang," said Cappy.

Their bus looked a few inches lower than customary. Then Viddy saw the reason. Factoryville's way of saying a so-long was to let air from their tires. All flat.

"Is this bad awful?" she asked Dawg.

69

Flashing a wet grin, he fetched her up to hold close, so they both could feel the rain pelting their young faces. "No, baby sister, even though some meany done this to us a purpose, there's nothing here we can't fix, laugh at, and motor away from. Sometimes life a flat tire, Vidalia. But remember, it only be flat on the bottom."

With a hand pump, it took time and turns, but the chore got itself did. A gentle summer rain, following the storm, seemed to rinse the dirty grit of Factoryville off everybody. A blessing of a bath, it was a warm shower from Heaven's watering can. Made her tended, Viddy thought, like a young garden flower. There must be somebody up in the sky, higher than a mist.

By the time the final tire had blossomed back to a solid circle of black, the rain stopped. Ethiopia's Clowns were smiling again. From above, merely a drop or two of water persisted, to remind them of a rainfall now complete. As the sky cleared, a rainbow could be seen, its curving arc of color bending a great hunter's bow. One of its stripes was bus purple.

For some reason, Cappy, who'd been blessed by the fairest voice, began to hum. No words. Yet his music, even though it was a hymn that Viddy had never heard, invited other voices. Then, one by each, almost all of the Clowns of Ethiopia Jones became a choir. Every man made his own humble hum, and the whole of it lofted gently upward as a grateful psalm of deliverance.

When their music stopped, it was quiet except for Cappy's voice. He seemed to want to sing some hymn words:

"Amazing grace, how sweet the sound,
That saved a wretch like me.
I once was lost, but now am found,
Was blind, but now I see."

Standing between Wash and Cappy, Viddy held hands with both of them, pretending, imagining that the pair of bent and graying men were something she'd never had to enjoy: a mother and a father.

Vidalia wasn't aware of which day it was. One thing sure, it rung sweeter than a Sunday-morning bell.

10

"PROCTORBURG," SANG WASH'S SOCIAL-DIRECTOR VOICE from behind the wheel. "Gentlemen, we's here about to de-bus at Proctorburg."

"With you navigationing," Cappy snorted, "a wonder we ain't stuck in a snowbank somewheres north of Alaska."

Yanking the *click-click-click* parking brake, Wash said, "Oh, we done pass through Alaska, one end t'other, while you copped a snooze. And them Eskimo ladies seem to recall your name, because they was all a hollering for *Blubber*."

"Vidalia," warned Cappy as he stretched to unkink his stilts and unclog his brain, "don't listen up too close at Mr. George Washington. It might maculate your mind."

While they were unloading from their purple bus, Wash commented that he was greatly relieved to say farewell to the last town, which was called Glade Spa. Even though the folks were all friendly, the field wasn't. Swizzlestick reported that center field had a mudhole the size to pleasure a herd of hogs.

The ballpark in Glade Spa was mere a meadow; beyond the outfield, there was no sign of a fence. Only miles of pasture. With her own eyes, Viddy had seen something not to be believed: Dawg, in right field, had somehow caught a deep fly ball after he bumped into a cow.

Hadn't been a whole lot safer for their fans. Behind home plate the chicken wire that screened off tipped fouls sported holes you could throw a cat through. Nobody do such, even though there were a dozen cats all over everywhere. A cat, however, didn't run away with a foul ball.

A dog did.

It was the only new baseball, so the game suspended while the umpire's wife drove home, at a clip, to bring back another one.

Proctorburg, some claimed, featured a far finer ballpark—and, best of all, a refreshment stand worthy of a county fair. Viddy was delighted, as were all the Clowns, to discover that the food stand was already open and hungry for paying customers.

A large redheaded gent who wore a clean white apron greeted a busload of Clowns with a welcoming grin. "Howdy! Glad to have you gents here. And we got ballpark chow that'll make yer feet dance up a jig and your belly sing *Dixie*. So what'll ya gonna eat?"

"Ladies first," said Cappy, bowing to Vidalia. Then he escorted her forward and lifted her up over the counter edge in order to see. Because the refreshment shack stocked so

73

much, and so many varieties of flavors, color, and smells, Viddy couldn't decide.

"A hot dog for our mascot," Wash piped up, "plus a Hershey bar and a root beer. Later, after she puts herself outside all that, maybe a box of that hot buttered popcorn."

Cappy ordered a cream soda, plus three dogs with chopped onions, mustard, relish, catsup, salt, and pepper. He called his mess "The Works." As it turned out, the mustard happened to taste extra-hot, so the large redheaded proprietor set him up an extra homemade sarsaparilla, for *free*.

"On the house."

When ol' Cappy reached for it, RED (according to his name tag) smiled knowingly, pointed at Cappy's beat-up right hand and said, "I see you're a catcher." He held up his own right with a few busted twigs imagining they were still fingers. "Me too. Catching sure is tough to play. With regard to difficulty, short is hardest. Best shortstop I ever saw was like you fellers, a person of Negro persuasion, whose name was Willie Wells. What a ballplayer! However, for all-around agony, behind the plate is gotta be roughest in pain."

"Not for Cappy," said Wash, "on account he clean misses at least a half of my artistic pitches. The rest he just drops or stops with his face."

"When you're fresh," the catcher retorted, "you might throw a fastball through a wet Kleenex. All that's keeping you on the mound is my smart signals and your saliva."

"Say," said RED, "you rascals needle each other worse'n two years ago. I remember now. You were telling us about some horrible happening y'all had north of here, over to Factoryville."

"Haven't been back in two years," said Wash, "and we ain't fixing a sudden visit."

"Well, it's got worse," RED told them. "For a spell, the steel mill was running two days a week, then one. Heard recent that it's shut for keepers." He shook his head. "Factoryville doesn't even field a baseball team no more."

"A pity," Cappy said. "A sorry shame."

Viddy figured that Cappy and Wash would be joysome over Factoryville's bad news. But neither man seemed to like the listening. They weren't men who could ha-ha somebody else going broke.

After the Ethiopia's Clowns got served eats, RED final wiped his freckled face with a paper towel, then paused to pour, roll, and lick a shaggy cigarette. "There's to be a special treat for everyone this afternoon. My wife, Bloomer, is honoring us with a musical solo."

"Do she sing?" Viddy asked.

"Often," said RED. "But today, before the game commences, Bloomer is going to render us a hymn."

"Oh," said Wash, "on a pump organ?"

"Nope. Bloom plays the sousaphone, the largest and most important contrivance in a brass band, invented by Mr. John Philip Sousa." RED's face became sad. "If he hadn't of *died* in 1932, he'd still be alive today."

Game time wasn't until three o'clock, yet ardent fans had filed into the grandstand. Not a seat left. Two lines of side-by-side cars parked along the baselines, home to first and home to third. Cautious drivers pulled their pane of windshield glass out of its stanchions, so it wouldn't shatter by a sliced foul ball. Or a pulled one.

Bloomer, carrying her giant silvery horn with a golden bell, stood at home plate, took several deep breaths, and louder than a war between foghorns, blasted and bombed the unholy Hell out of *Whispering Hope*.

Bowing, she exited to applause.

"Who that little gent coming?" Viddy asked Wash.

"Oh, that there a heck of a good guy. Mr. Hydrant Harry Hyde, owner of our hosts, the Proctorburg Pirates." Wash leaned closer to Viddy's ear. "He also a prosperous local agent for the H. J. Heinz Company of Pittsburgh."

Harry shook hands with Cappy and Wash. He was taller than a red fire hydrant, Vidalia noticed, but not by much.

"Mr. Ethiopia Jones and Mr. Washington," he said, "welcome back to our fine and friendly town. Since we last met, our Pirates have rightly improved. We signed up a few hotshots, and we take twice-a-week batting practice. So do us a favor, gents. *Don't let us win!* If we beatcha, we want to do it square, on the up-and-up. Our umpire gets a good fee. And I got Jimmy's solemn promise that he'll call 'em fair."

Cappy nodded.

"Sounds good," Wash told him.

Looking up at both their faces, the little gentleman beamed and again shook their hands.

"Let's play ball!"

For Viddy, it promised to be a beautiful day because something jim-dandy happened. A little white girl, about her size, stood near their dugout, holding a baseball, old and useless, its horsehide cover torn off. Nothing more than a lump of twine.

"Look what I found," she told Viddy. "I'll roll it to you, if'n you roll it back." Knees bending, she stooped to the ground. "Will ya?"

Never having had a playmate her own age, Vidalia didn't know what to mention or do, except to delight in it all. To her surprise, the little white girl smiled her way.

"My name is Tildee." The girl waited. "I don't guess you got a name, or you'd speak it out to me."

"Vidalia."

It felt so strange to be telling her name to another child, a little white person who wanted to play with her. It was near as happy as hearing mockingbirds, even when the girl said that her name was Tildee Tully and then asked Viddy what her other name be.

"Vidalia is all I got." She smiled. "But sometimes Wash and Cappy calls me Viddy." She almost laughed. "So I s'pose I be Viddy Vidalia."

"Who's Wash and Cappy? Your ma and pa?"

"No. They's my battery."

It was sporty to roll the ball along on the bumpy ground. Tildee sended it to her and then Viddy'd shoot it right back again. Sometimes a loop of string would come loose and then they would re-wrap the lumpy ball; as they worked together, their hands would touch, almost the way Cappy, as captain, shook hands with home-team managers or bosses. Rolling the ball was nice, but what Vidalia liked best was when their hands meeted, and their fingers became friends.

The little game didn't take up hardly no room at all, because they only rolled the used baseball a few feet. They weren't making noise, only giggles. Not hurting nobody. Why, Viddy wondered, was the white woman angry? The look on the lady's face seemed to grow so ugly mean and almost spitted out sorry when she snapped at her little girl.

"Tildee, don't you know no better'n to strike up with . . . certain people? They ain't like us. Can't you *see*?"

After the woman kicked the ball away, she took a hold on Tildee's arm, cuffed her face, and made her cry. Then the woman hauled the girl off out of sight. Viddy stood alone, wondering what was so wrong about rolling a ball and laughing up fun. She didn't feel hungry.

Just empty.

11

IT WAS A CLOSE GAME.

"Hydrant Harry Hyde didn't deal us no jive," said Cappy, groaning himself up and into their bus, "because his Pirates can really rally."

"That young apple-cheek pitcher," Wash Washington said, "ain't no Dizzy Dee or Satchel, but he throwed heat, and a arsenal of breaking stuff. At the plate, with a bat in my hands, I was cogitating a curve, down and away, and he screws one at me. Near clipped off my belt buckle. Can't complain, 'cause I be leaning at least a inch into the zone."

Spitting out a open bus window, Cappy said, "Well, we managed to beat 'em, but only by a run."

"Don't matter, Cap. What I do rejoice at here in Proctorburg is simple this. Regardless of who makes a good play in the field, or clouts, home team or visitors or black or white, the crowd put hands together and clap."

Cappy nodded. "You are right, W.W. Any bunch of no-counts can root for their own team or razz visitors, but when a fan honks his car horn to homage another team's homer, I call it prime-rib baseball."

"Yeah," agreed Wash. "That feller's a sport."

Grinding its gears, and with Junebug behind the wheel, the purple bus of Ethiopia's Clowns pulled out of the Proctorburg ballpark, heading for the open road. To their surprise, several people of varying pigmentation waved to them. One elderly white gentleman called out, "Y'all come back now. Hear?"

"We certain will," hollered Catfish, and Junebug tooted the fellow a double salute on the bus horn.

"Not a single sorry soul in this entire town," said Hookworm, their fleet thirdsacker, who'd earned his nick-name by an ability to hook-slide and avoid a tag.

"Nope," agreed Dawg, "nary a one. I never seen or heared nobody say, or do, ugly."

Right then, little Viddy spoke out. "But a woman slap Tildee."

"Who?"

"Tildee's mama. She up'n cuff her awful mean in the face. Make her cry. Turn me so dreadful I near run after 'em to ask the white lady why. All we doing is play a back-and-fro with a ball. No harm done." Viddy folded her skinny arms. "Don't reason."

In low voices, several of the Clowns repeated what Viddy said. Each player who heard the whisper seemed to sadden. Catfish hang his head. What she'd told Dawg got passed through the entire bus, eventual to Junebug, who be trying to drive. He didn't cuss, yet his hands tighten on the wheel like he wanted to hurt it.

The happiness drained from Dawg's face. "Hook," he said, "bail me out. What we tell our child?"

Hookworm kissed Viddy's hand. "Lord," he then said, "ya didn't make this black boy strong enough."

Viddy said, "I don't savvy."

Hookworm and Dawg looked at each other as if neither knew what to say or do next. Dawg shrugged his shoulders and then spoke. "Girl, they's plenty in this ol' world I don't yet savvy, and whatever I can't understand, I try not to mess with."

Hook agreed. "For sure, living can be a mystery. No place perfect. And this boy ain't about to pack up, git, and return to old Africa. No way. I'd guess we don't begin to be aware how awful life is across the big drink. And me, I ain't willing to venture a find-out. Not under no black slave trader."

"Me neither," said Dawg. "I just sort of wants my age to make it all the way to eighteen."

With a sly smile on his handsome young face, Hookworm looked at Viddy; his finger poked her ribs to a snicker. Nobody said anything more. Viddy, fed up with questioning, decided to close her eyes and permit their bus to jiggle her asleep, hoping she might have a nice dream about playing with Tildee. No sooner, however, had she filled her lungs, then let out a big breath of wind, when a distant noise prevented her from sleeping.

It sounded like a fire truck.

Whatever it was, the sound grew louder from behind; Nap and Tonic were looking out of the bus's rear seat, one pointing, the other making a curious face.

"June," a voice yelled forward to Junebug, "you best ease up that gas pedal. We got us a po-lice car back yonder, and it gaining."

As their bus slowed, Viddy rushed to the back-end window and wedged herself between Nap and Tonic to see a flashing red light on a black car.

"You stop," Cappy told Junebug, "or we resisting arrest."

Junebug halted to a whoa. The siren retarded its scream to quiet, and a pair of men jumped out. One was wearing a policeman's uniform. The other wasn't, and at once Viddy recognized him as the little owner of the Proctorburg Pirates, none other than the short Mr. Hydrant Harry Hyde. When Junebug yanked the long bar of a door opener, the bus admitted Mr. Hyde, who was carrying a brown paper bag.

"Sorry," said Junebug, "if I was over hasty."

"Not at all," laughed a jovial Mr. Hyde.

"What's troubling?" Wash, who'd been asleep, was eager to learn. Yawning, he rubbed a tired eye and stretched.

Standing to greet their boarder, Cappy held out a hand, which Mr. Hyde shook. "We didn't break no law in Proctorburg, did we?"

"No indeedy. Nothing of the kind. You aces aren't in any kind of Dutch, so relax. All I wanted to tell you good baseballers is this. My cousin, her name is Gertrude Evans, happened to be attending today's game, back yonder at the ballpark. Saw a particular scene that made her boil. When we final ran into each other, Gertie filled me in on the entire shebang, how one of our citizens was cantankery. Downright rude." Mr. Hyde hauled in a breath. "We wanted your young lady to know that if certain people lack the good breeding to apologize, someone else had better pitch in. There's plenty of southern gentility in Proctorburg. And hospitality."

"Well, I'll be," said Hookworm.

"May I please inquire," Mr. Hyde asked, "the name of your special and adorable little mascot here?"

"Her name's Vidalia," said Cappy.

With a quick tug, Mr. Hyde extracted a large-size glass jar of pickles out of the paper bag, handing it to Viddy. "A modest token," he said, "from Mr. H. J. Heinz to you, personal."

"It mine?"

Mr. Hyde nodded.

"You betcha. And we haven't seen anything yet," he said, fumbling into a coat pocket to produce a little white box. "The pickles are for you, Vidalia, to pass out to your teammates, for all to partake. But *this*," he said, handing her the box, "is only for *you* to wear. Your very own private piece of jewelry. Open 'er up."

Removing the top, Viddy saw something green inside. It was a tiny pickle, made of metal, and about an inch long, with five white letters printed across it.

HEINZ

"It's a pickle pin," Mr. Hyde said. "Every time you choose to wear it, why, you can be reminded of all your friends in Proctorburg." He sighed. "I know it's not much. But on the spur of the moment, in haste, all I could think of to bring was this little green smile."

"Thank the man," said Cappy. "Please."

She couldn't speak.

"Shy," whispered Wash. "A mite shy."

"Thank you, mister," Viddy said.

"Good girl," Cappy said. "See? We done our level best to shine her some, with decent raising."

"You're welcome, Vidalia. Now, if you'll please permit, I shall pin this brooch to your dress, right up under your chin and to one side, where you'll be able to glance down and see it smiling up at you."

All the Clowns clapped.

A moment later, Mr. Hyde exited from the purple bus and returned to the police patrol car, which turned around and headed back toward Proctorburg. But it was several minutes before Junebug even attempted to start the engine. Alas, it wouldn't fire.

"You flooded it again," said Catfish. "Take your fooly foot off'n the pedal and let 'er breathe a spell."

"Boys," said Cappy, "know how I feel? Well, kind of like champagne. But, for right now, I do believe I might be convinced to settle for a pickle."

"Me too," said Wash Washington.

The jar's lid was screwed on too snug for Viddy to loosen, so Dawg helped. But alone, she walked the aisle to pass a pickle to everyone. All the boys admired her pin and then munched a crisp green treat.

"Never," said Dawg, "do I ever taste a pickle sweet as this'n." He grinned. "Like a particular baby onion I know."

12

"WE GOT ROBBED," CAPPY SAID.

"How come," asked Wash, leaning on a purple fender, "you's mentioning a robbery at me?"

"Account," said Cappy, "the robber female."

"Go way."

"You listen up, fool, while I information you some." He leveled a finger at the pitcher's chest. "Her name be sort of a Lucy."

"Who is?"

"A scarlet woman, who call herself Loosey Caboose. Many's the time we hear a freight train in these up-north parts, wailing in the night, and rumbling over a grade crossing. Last car usual a dusty red. Not this caboose. Madam Loosey's be such a fire red that you'll require smoke glasses to behold it."

"You tryin' to boogie me?" Wash asked.

"Nope. Every summer, on the D and H . . ."

"What's that?"

"It stand for the Delaware and Hudson Railroad, Incorporated. Anyhow, there's a spur line serving a few Adirondack towns that do lumber and some paper mills."

"Cappy, what is all such about?"

"Loosey Caboose, who just happen to be a plump and pleasing high-yella gal, dedicated to spreading . . . *joy* to whoever might cotton to indulge in seeking her coffee-colored company."

Viddy, who was hiding nearby and not able to understand even a single and solitary sentence, was all ears. For quite a spell, Vidalia had been fascinated by trains, especially when, in the dark of night, that lonesome tin whistle warned that an engine was approaching, hauling freight through one small sleepy town and headed toward the next.

"This ol' Loosey Caboose gal, she rob us?"

Cappy nodded. "Wash, we short five players. Mostly our kids. Nonetheless, we got to pile on the omnibus, head south, and recruit us enough talent to tally up to nine. Right now, we are pitiful short. Not counting Vidalia, we got exactly a sum of four. Do you expect us to meander into Chestertown, New York, and field a pitcher and catcher plus two?"

"It ain't comfortable," Wash said, "to exist down south and play baseball in a June temperature. Even though the north people ain't as friendly."

Cappy grinned.

"Nor," he stated, "is it comfort to chug this'n here bus to a town and tell 'em we got four against their nine. Come on,

Wash. I don't imagine what it is you smoking, but it ain't Lucky Strike. We either field a team, or we hightail straight out of here and then due south, to where we locate a few young coons to hurl, hit, and hustle bases."

"Know how you're sounding, Ethiopia?"

"How?"

"Like a Boston slave-ship captain."

"If so, I do regret, Mr. Washington. I confess that I'm mere efforting to hold my Clowns together. You included. All I be, Wash, is a aging fat catcher, knees shot, legs that couldn't outleg Grandmother Grunt down a line to first. I'm hurting so dreadful that I ought to bat ninth in the order and let you, a pitcher, hit number eight."

Wash said, "I know, Cap."

"Do you, brother?"

"Honest. When I'm out there on the mound and there's nobody on base, I been noticing how ya catch. On one knee."

"Can't bamboozle you, can I, Wash?"

"Not me. You don't jive me none. We been a battery for too many years, Ethiopia. It's be you and me, sixty feet apart, and yet side by side."

Cappy punched him an easy shot.

Wash yawned. "Okay, who gone?"

"Tonic, Hookworm, Catfish, Nap, and Swizzlestick. Where they be? I can only guess that they're enjoying a ride behind a freight train, along with a few horizontal hospitalities of Miss Loosey Caboose."

"I can't believe all this, Cappy."

"Know it, bro. So climb behind that wheel, Mr.

Washington, and point this purple and half-vacant vehicle in a southernly direction. I'll spell ya. And we ain't fixing to stop, except for gas, until we reach Virginia."

"Leastwise," said Junebug, "they left us their uniforms."

"Oh," sang Wash, "I wish I was in the land o' cotton. Here up north they treat me rotten, get away, go astray, in the hay, Dixieland."

For almost two days they rode south, pausing to pick up to-go meals. Mile after mile, Viddy grew sadder and sadder, figuring she wouldn't ever again see their missing players.

In Norfolk, they bunked at a place Cappy had heard of, sort of a agency for Negro ballplayers who itched to play and were willing to travel. Almost every day there were tryouts. Most of the candidates were about Dawg's age, a few even younger.

"Balance," said Cappy. "The kids are fresher'n paint, but we require a few veterans to daddy our babes."

After a day and a half, Ethiopia's Clowns signed on five new ballplayers: three kids and two tough chestnuts. The youngsters: Shank, Mudpuddle, and Lullaby. Two experienced infielders: Sugarbeet Johnson and Sid Granville, whose nickname was Granny.

Wash wasn't so certain, but their captain, Mr. Ethiopia Jones, convinced him that the changes added up to a stronger nine.

Along with new players came a fresh problem. Five of them. The baseball uniforms didn't fit. Viddy, who for the past year had become handy with needle and thread, started to measure with a string, cut, and stitch. She worked all during the daylight, and beyond, when Cappy warned her she'd ruin her eyesight. Yet she final did it. Five uniforms, and all five close to fitting proper.

The new players thanked her more'n once for doing such a tidy job in so short a time.

The Clowns did something in Norfolk that little Viddy had never seen them do. They practiced. Two young out-fielders were both fleet and eager, Shankbone in left, Mud in right, with Dawg's speed now in center. And all three could timber the ball, steal, and slide.

"At second," Cappy told her, "that new youngster will prove okay. Yup, I do like the way Lullaby works with our short, Junebug. We have a tight and quick middle infield. At third, Sugarbeet's got soft hands on either wing, plus a strong and on-target arm to make the long throw."

"Cap," Viddy asked, "at first base, you think Granny'll work out good as Tonic?"

"Better."

"How come?"

"Promise you won't tell Wash?"

Viddy nodded. "I promise, Cappy."

"Well," he said, "at first base, Tonic made a number of faulty choices. Whenever a ball's popped up between home and first, I want my firstsacker to scamper at a full-out gallop and hog that ball. Because all I got is a catcher's mitt, and if the pop's moving away, the firsty's got a better bead on it." Cappy gave Viddy a squeeze. "As to choice, if they got a runner on first and a grounder rolled to Tonic's right, he'd play the ball, whirl, and then throw to old turtle-foot

Wash covering first instead of the easier left-handed peg to second, where Junebug would nip the lead runner."

"Wash can cover first base."

"Years ago, certain. But for a pitcher of Mr. Washington's years, he ain't always reliable to break for the bag soon enough. Then he's got to catch a throw and touch ahead of a runner. Wash can't always make the play."

"Granny'll play better'n Tonic?"

"Seems so. Only time'll tell. Tonic is younger, but something tells me that Granny will tighten our infield a turn or two. Speed's one element. But at first base, a brain is more of an asset than a cleat."

"Tonic was good."

"And a lot of years more youthful than Granny. But hesitating. Granny'll know quick what to do, when to field or cover the bag. I had a talk with him, and before I could suggest it, Granny had sized up both Junebug and Wash. He told me that if a runner was on first and a bunt lay down, he'd almost always try to throw to Junebug at second rather than to Wash hobbling toward first."

Viddy reached over to touch Cappy's right hand and all its uneven fingers. "You certain do know a plenty about baseball. How did ya savvy so much?"

"Years. Game after game. If you observe, Vidalia, you'll learn. Absorb. Soak in all the information that's out there happening every second on that diamond of dirt."

"Tell me some more stuff, Cappy, 'cause I want to learn all I can."

"Okay, pet. In a batting lineup, our star base-stealer ought to get followed by a smart veteran, a patient hitter who'll take enough pitches for our runner on first to study the pitcher, then steal. A too-eager kid won't do such."

"What else?"

"Well, both middle infielders have to relay a deep-hitted ball. Take the throw from a outfielder, turn, and fire a frozen string to the plate."

"I got it. Gimme one more thing to remember."

"All right. When I'm scouting a prospective young and right-handed outfielder, I judge if he catch a fly ball close to his right shoulder, so he's quick ready to peg."

Viddy smiled. "I'm glad we're final fixed up proper. Do we got ourselfs a perfect ball club?"

Cappy sighed. "Except for pitcher and catcher."

13

IT WAS 1939 AND A NEW SEASON.

"This is it," Wash moaned. "Maybe it change our luck."

"Where we be, Mr. Washington?" their new right fielder, Mudpuddle, wanted to know. "Where we come to?"

"Florida, my boy. Mud, please quit calling me Mr. Washington, on account I don't cotton to spook poor Martha. I'm plain Wash."

Trying to wipe a dirty bus window to see outside, Viddy didn't think that Florida looked a whole different than Alabama. Same bunkers of red clay, run-over dogs in the road, and up-above buzzards drawing their slow black circles around a hot sky. For the past month, neither Georgia nor Alabama had earned the team much money. A few dollars here and there.

Viddy hoped Florida would prove fatter.

Since she could recollect, the Clowns had never struck it

rich, and this year showed no boom of improvement.

"Are we still in Depression?"

Wash chuckled. "Sugar child, we's so broke-down busted that we don't recognize the Depression even if it jump up and pinch our bottoms." He tickled her to a laugh. "Go back yonder and stir up Cappy. If he's sober, reward him a kiss. But if he's otherwise, knock his knees together. That'll alert the ol' backstop."

While the bus was rolling and bumping through Florida, it wasn't too easy to stagger back through the aisle to the rear. Yet, by holding on to one sleeping ballplayer after another, Viddy managed.

"Cappy?"

No answer. As she leaned closer, she could smell the sorry of his breath, a mixture of chaw tobacco and stale whiskey. A empty bottle lay beside him. It hurt to see his fingers gripping glass, like he had nothing else to hang on to.

"Cap." She nudged him. "You awake?"

Braving the sour stench of his breathing, Viddy rested her head on his mound of a chest. He felt almost too hot to be near. When the bus bumped over a pothole, her face rubbed against his chin's beard stubble, an army of tiny white swords, worse than a pricker bush.

Another jolt of the bus disturbed him enough to mumble something. His arm crept around her shoulders and held her closer. It felt so friendly good, like the Cappy she'd known for ten years, a man she had seen grow so fat and feeble.

Sometimes she'd actual pretend that she honest got born

94

as Miss Vidalia Jones, the daughter of Mr. Ethiopia Jones, captain of a baseball team.

His right hand no longer looked like a hand, more like a beat-up mitt, fingers split by foul tips and Wash's into-the-dirt sinkers. Cappy's hand had become a twisted tangle of swollen knuckles, short lengths of knotted rope that could hardly hold a baseball, unable to really wing it. Cappy Jones was the only man ever to catch Wash Washington. All of those pitches, outs, innings, games, double-headers, seasons, through summers up north and winters down south.

Then all of those bottles.

During the last few years, Cappy held on only because of the secret swigs in the dugout. At first, he drank on the sly, whenever the Clowns were batting; then after a while he didn't seem to bother who notice.

"I need it," Cappy had once tried to explain, lifting her to his lap. "It's my crutch, pie baby. Because unless I'm oiled, these ol' legs don't function."

Game after game, Viddy had begun to realize that his need was something more than knee thirst. Cut off his legs, and he'd still crave it until their last few dollars spent for a bottle.

No one asked him to quit.

In a sense, the Clowns were entire aware that the booze was killing him. So, in silence, they watched him die, knowing that baseball was his life; being unable to play might be more painful than a retirement death. Thus they all allowed their veteran catcher to try to catch whatever was slipping away.

95

"My God, my God," Viddy whispered to his unhearing ear, Bible words that Cappy had taught her before his sickness. "Why hast thou forsaken me?" Then she sang to him, very quietly. "Jesus, lover of my soul, let me to thy bosom fly."

Cappy had taught the hymn to her, long ago.

Close to his face, the beard was a briar, yet Viddy stayed with him, close as she could cuddle. His hair was a mussed-up thatch of angry wool, intent on rebellion. Best she could, her hand stroked Cappy's silvery hair again and again.

"Sleep," she whispered. "I be the mama, and you's my little boy child, tired out, worn to bone." She giggled. "My, you awful big for a dolly."

Somewhere in the team bus Viddy kept a bucket and rags. Before a game she'd beg a match from Granny or Sugarbeet, both of whom smoked, in order to start a wee fire out of twigs. After warming the bucket water, she wrapped the heated rags around Cappy's hand and both swollen knees.

These were her rules to keep him catching: Heat before a game. Ice after.

For some time, Cappy had been telling her how much it aided him, chasing away the hurt. Yet not enough to forgo a slug of hootch.

Raising her head from his shirtfront, Viddy carefully removed the glass whiskey bottle from his hand. THREE FEATHERS, the label said. GENUINE BLENDED WHISKEY. A window was open. She tossed the bottle outside, clear of the gravel roadway, so the glass wouldn't shatter and shred up somebody's tires.

"I hope you break up," she told the departing Three Feathers. "And I wish every bottle them people make gits busted, to let the poison ooze out, so other peoples don't go sickly, like Cappy."

Cautious not to wake him, Viddy rubbed his right hand, very gentle, to bring it back to life. Closing her eyes, she remembered how Cappy once could peg to second. Nap covering. Like a bullet, the ball would fire right smack to his waiting glove, a few inches above second base. Perfect to tag a stealer, and he usual be out by a couple of strides. Slide right into the ball that was waiting between the sack and his upper straight-out leg.

"Nap," she sighed, "I wonder where you at now, these days. Gone somewhere on a train with a red-caboose lady. Never see you no more. Because now, at second base, we got Lullaby."

What be the name of the town they headed at? Viddy couldn't recall. Only that it had a plenty of sounds in it. Earlier, one of the players had told her its name, but she'd forgotten. Just one more sorry little town, her mind pictured, with a turpentine mill, orange trees, or a cattle butchery. And faces. A lot more empty faces of people who didn't have jobs. No bread on their tables. Needless to say, in their pockets there wouldn't be enough jingle for the price of a ticket into the ballpark.

Just yesterday, or possible it was the day before, Wash had made a remark about hard times. "These days," he'd said, "I don't guess that over a dozen baseball fans would cough up a price to watch Satchel Paige pitch to Josh Gibson."

97

"Who?" she'd asked Wash.

"Oh, only two of the primest players that ever held a horsehide." Wash had lifted her up to straddle his thigh, like a pony ride. "Somehow, I'd certain enjoy taking you to watch how those men play the game. Like they invented it."

"Are they better than the Clowns?"

"Oh, in some matters. Better gloves. Our team only owns one bat. But those boys, why there's a length of lumber for each player. And clean uniforms for every game. Don't imagine that their team bus resemble our poor ol' chugger. Add to that, they probable git paid on time. Girl, the big teams git paid in advance, before they run out into the heat."

"Wash, do you wish you be one of them?"

The pitcher grinned.

"Nope. No way. Wanna know why I'm so chesty proud to play for Ethiopia's Clowns? I got me a very special reason."

"Tell me."

"Them big teams," he'd said, "maybe got a bunch of frills and fancy, but there's one special item they don't got. And never will."

"What's that?"

Wash hugged her. "You."

For a spell, the pitcher was quiet and seemed to be working on something special to say. Wash turned to look at her serious. "Promise me, Viddy. Promise you'll remember Cappy to the very end of your life, no matter how olden you grow. Just sort of try to remember all us busted-up old Clowns. Because what you be, girl, is sort of our scrapbook."

She had nodded.

These were Vidalia's memories as the bus coughed along a gritty road, on its way to another griddle-hot game. With her face resting on the dampness of Cappy's shirt, she held a swollen and crippled hand, listening to the heavy labor of his breathing. Eyes slowly closing, Viddy allowed the moving bus to rock her asleep. She slept close to her catcher until she was awakened by Wash's hollering, from the driver's seat, announcing the name of the place where they'd arrived.

"Callahoochee."

14

"I CAN PLAY," CAPPY INSISTED.

It was coming up two o'clock in steamy Florida, and the temperature was so hot that breathing cooked your lungs. While helping Cappy to buckle on his chest protector and shin guards, Viddy was praying that he'd not have to bat very often.

"Hey, I'm able," Cappy kept on saying, as though trying to sell himself into believing it.

Nobody, nary a one of the other eight players, told him he couldn't. Not even Wash. Yet, from what Viddy could observe, all of their faces hung silent, cautioning him to stay in the dugout. Cancel the game. Anything to keep their catcher captain under shade.

A hand over his eyes, squinting at a sun-baked ball diamond, Wash said, "Be a oven out yonder, heating up to fry every fool who thinks he can gallop through it and not

100

roast." He glanced over at Cap. "Especial a couple o' has-beens like us."

Thumping a fist into the worn leathery pocket of his mitt, Cappy said, "This game of baseball is all I know. Everything I do since before I growed up."

Noticing a loose rawhide lace in the webbing of his catcher's mitt, Viddy snugged it tighter, trying to retie the frayed thongs. In her fingers, those two short lengths felt life-less; she tried not to think about how close they resembled Cappy and Wash. How many more games could these dried-out lumps of leather play?

Like usual, top of the first, the visiting Clowns were at bat. Sugarbeet led off and fanned. With a careless excuse-me swing, Mud popped up. Dawg rapped a single but then got tagged out trying for two.

Three up and three down cheered the crowd.

"Here we go, boys," Cappy barked in his customary way, and he grunted up from the dugout bench, ambling to the plate. "Let's look like a heads-up club. Talk up the chatter out there."

Following a few of Wash Washington's tosses, Viddy saw that Cappy didn't bother to practice a throw to second. Instead, he merely lobbed a floater back to the mound, wiped his sweaty face with a sleeve, yanked down the mask, and awaited the opposing lead-offer.

The Callahoochee All-Stars was a white team of young men, tan, tawny, a well-coached club.

Earlier, they had fielded smoothly, exchanging fluid throws, and moved with confident speed. As the game progressed, they hit solidly, as Wash's hook didn't seem to be breaking. Viddy could tell by the sound their bats made. Sharp cracks. The woody echo usually rang for an instant. Chimes of ash.

Top of the third.

This meant, for Ethiopia's Clowns, a bottom trio of their batting order, the three oldest members: Granny, Wash (hitting eighth instead of ninth), and Cappy.

Granny went with an outside curve, neatly pushing the ball over short for a single. At first he only took a modest turn toward second, retreated, then rested a tired left foot on a ledge of the bag. Wash bunted and got thrown out, but his sacrifice advanced Granny to second. Scoring position.

"Bring him in," Shank said to Cappy as the catcher picked up their only bat where Wash had discarded it and approached the plate. The Clowns hooted out support.

"You'll do it, Cap."

"Okay okay okay. Everybody hit."

Next to Viddy on the dugout bench, Wash cupped his hands to holler, "Come on, Cappy, be a hitter up there. Show 'em how to clobber." Turning to Viddy, he said, "Thank the blessed goodness that old codger swings righthanded, so his left can supply most of the force. Using a golf club's the same style. Your right hand, so they tell me, just sort of guides the power to the left."

"Is that real, Wash?"

"Real and truly, sweet pea."

Even though it was dry weather, no mud, Cappy moved the plate, stopped, then knocked the imaginary dirt off his cleats. Stooping, he scooped up sand to rub along the bat handle. Then, once in the batter's box, he tugged his cap tighter and wiggled his back foot, the right, to dig in a stance.

"Now ain't he a showman," Wash said proudly. "Give our coot some credit. Most of what you're watching, Vidalia, is an excuse to keep their pitcher a few minutes longer on that hill of heat. If you don't believe it's dreadful hot out there, feel my shirt. Already wet clear to bone."

"A stall?"

Wash nodded. "Yep, to allow all of his teammates a few extra moments of sublime dugout shade." Wash let out a sigh. "That pathetic lush shouldn't be out there at all."

As Cappy took a few practice swings across the plate, someone in the grandstand hooted at him. "Quit all the dramatics, Fatty, and pretend you can play ball. We don't got all weekend."

This one afternoon, Viddy thought, is maybe all Cappy's got to give. Covering her eyes, she hoped he could go nine. Looking out on the field again, she saw Cappy take a pitch, high and inside, holding the bat above his head with his left hand, allowing the ball to breeze his beard by only inches.

"Ball one," the umpire called.

Cappy grinned and took another. A bit outside, yet the local ump knew where bread's buttered and called it a strike. The next pitch was fatter and across the meat of the plate. Cap swung late and fouled it off.

Wash shook his head. "Ten years ago, girl, Mr. Jones would've swatted that apple out of the orchard. He's lost his timing. Plus a fact he ought to wear cheaters. You know, glasses."

"Can't he see?" Viddy asked.

"Sometimes. But lately, when he's working behind the plate, he can't focus the mitt as he catches my throws. The sound tells me, because the ball don't plunk the pocket dead middle. Yup, the off-center muffy noise tells me a whole sad story."

Sitting there swinging her dirty feet, Viddy was hoping Wash Washington might be wrong, and she didn't cotton to hear any more about Cappy's not being fit to play baseball. Yet she knew that Wash wasn't jiving. He talked righteous. Ethiopia Jones could no longer throw, hit, or catch a ball. Not like he used to. Realizing so tightened her fingers on the bench's rough edge.

Cappy hit a heater!

There was a sudden and sharp smack of lumber whacking horsehide, and it prompted Granny to break from second, turn third on the sack's inside corner, and leg it for home. Seeing it was a double, Granny merely coasted along the chalk. In the outfield, the well-tagged ball sailed through the gap between center and right, bouncing, then slowly rolling toward a right-center fence.

"Hold up," Wash was hollering.

Cappy, hungry for an extra base, rounded second with an eager eye for third.

"My, my, look at that warhorse fly," Wash said. "Golly to goodness, the fool's fixing to try for three. Runs slower, but, by jingle, maybe he still can play the game. Wow! He clubs a inside-out double and thinks he's Cool Papa Bell on the pads."

Meanwhile, their secondsacker, who had moved deeper into right-center, gloved the relay, pivoted, and fired a perfect peg. Halfway to third, Cappy figured he was a dead duck; he halted, whirled, and retreated toward second. A throw beat him, but Cappy wasn't quite through. If they wanted an out, they'd have to run him down, which they did, easily, yet it took a few tosses to make the tag.

All grin because he'd knocked in a run with an extra-base hit, the slugger decided to keep on showing off. He sprinted at full blast toward the dugout as though telling the crowd he still had spunk.

But he didn't make it.

The happiness on his wrinkled face hardened to a grimace of pain, forcing his eyes to close. As his hand grabbed the place on his shirt that covered his heart, Cappy pitched forward, falling facedown into the grassless grit. Soon as Wash rolled him over, partly into shade, Viddy could see Cappy's eyes and mouth were open, but he wasn't talking. Or even blinking.

"I fetch a ambulance," Dawg offered.

"No," said Wash. "Cappy ain't to cash in his chips in some hospital, among doctors. Toss me his mitt."

He slipped it on Cappy's catching hand, his left, then slapped a baseball into its pocket.

"Why you do that?" Viddy asked Wash, brushing some grains of sand off Cappy's sweaty face.

"Girl, he's got a purchase on his life." Wash's arms briefly held her close. "Go give him a good-bye kiss, but don't pity him a speck. Just realize his day's all done. This is exact how he wanted to end, and now good ol' Cappy be going to a shadier rest."

Wash could barely speak.

Tenderly leaning on the burning barrel of Cappy's chest, Viddy heard his lungs release his life. Only once, and then Mr. Ethiopia Jones no longer reeked of tobacco or whiskey. Instead he was all leather, salty padding, and pure catcher.

With her head bowed, eyes shut, she inhaled his final breath to hold inside and to keep forever.

15

"Mockingbirds," said Vidalia, hearing their welcome to morning in the live oak trees south of the manor.

Beside her, Tate blinked at a brightening eastern sky and masked a yawn. "Sorry, Aunt Vidalia. I'm not bored. No way. I'm filled with your childhood. Bases loaded."

"Did I talk your ears off? Mind, I'm not regretful, as my story's ripe to tell, and time had come for you to listen."

"All those years," he said. "Long ago. Yet I vividly picture you, that innocent little girl wearing a grin, a raggy dress, and a pickle pin." Quickly, he glanced at her. "Do you still have it?"

Vidalia slowly nodded. "Yes indeed. If any chattel can be cherished . . . well, you already know. That pin is kept in a tiny box, top drawer of my dresser. Only piece of jewelry I own."

"You never wear any."

"But please see that I'm buried with it."

"I will. Count on it." He paused to reflect. "By the way, what exactly happened after Cappy died?"

Primly seated in the white wicker rocker, Vidalia leisurely stretched before answering.

"A plenty. Both teams crowded around. The white boys were so sweet, their faces as downcast as ours. The older players, and a lot in the crowd, had known Cappy many seasons. However, one of their youngest, an outfielder, knelt beside me to say he was sorry, asking me if Cappy was my granddaddy. Wash told him I had no folks. Just a team. And the finish of Ethiopia Jones meant the end of the Clowns. We were homeless, and our bus didn't run."

"I'm guessing who the young outfielder was."

"He said his name was Abbott and asked me mine. His pretty wife, Lavinia, joined us. The two whispered a bit, and then she said if nobody could look after me, she'd volunteer. Until they located me a suitable home."

"You wanted to stay with Wash?"

"When he told me that he was too olden and broke to raise me proper, I wanted to die alongside Cappy." Vidalia lowered her eyes. "Saying good-bye to men like George Washington and Ethiopia Jones isn't a snap."

"Yet you gritted your teeth and did it."

"Had to. Mr. Abbott and Miss Lavinia were so dear, bundling me into their beat-up Ford, first car I ever rode. A chariot to carry me home. My first home. Your great-grandfather washed my feet, then his bride thoroughly stripped and bathed me, fixed me a clean bed. Somehow I escaped into sleep."

Tate touched her hand. "I'm glad, Aunt Vidalia." As though holding her hand wasn't adequate, he rose to stand behind her chair, lightly resting his head to hers. "I'm so happy A.B. was there. Had they not acted promptly, our family might have missed a most worthy treasure." He paused, placing both hands on her shoulders. "And that's when they adopted you?"

Her hand touched one of his.

"Oh, not sudden. Mr. Abbott and Miss Lavinia tried to place me with my own race. Remember, this was about 1939 or 1940. The Great Depression. Households, black or white, couldn't afford another mouth to feed. Mr. Abbott finally located a black doctor and his wife who were interested. I recall his entering the kitchen with the news, yet not appearing overly pleased." Vidalia smiled. "However, by then, Miss Lavinia and I were belonging. And she delivered quite a speech."

"What did she say to A.B.?"

"She said something like *Abbott, this is my baby. A month ago, I already lost one child, and I'm not prepared to lose another. If I turn out unable to bear my own, it shall destroy me to live without Viddy.*"

"And what did Great-Granddad say?"

"Only one word."

"Tell me."

"*Ours.*"

A moment passed. And then Vidalia felt Tater kissing her hair, softly, silently; he also was rocking her chair, ever so lightly, as a daddy might rock a child. Resting her eyes,

Vidalia gave thanks that Mr. Tate's young life had somehow been spared, perhaps even chosen by a mystical spirit.

Gratefulness, she was thinking, surely sings the highest note in the hymn of prayer.

Behind her, so close that they could almost share breathing, stood her child. As well as belonging to Mr. Abbott, he was equally *hers*. Vidalia knew she now bore within her soul a child she never carried in her womb, a babe who'd never suckled at her breast.

Yet soon, he would nurse from her mind.

"Tater," she whispered.

"It was fascinating," he said, still rocking her chair an inch or two, "learning about Ethiopia and the baseball team. I'm trying to envision a battered bus."

"Color it purple."

"Why that?"

"Purple is a regal color."

"A king's robe?"

"Quite. Oddly enough, the black man didn't have social status, yet beknighted himself by painting his property purple and drinking Royal Crown Cola mixed with Seven Crown rye. Musicians called themselves Duke Ellington, Count Basie, or Nat King Cole."

Tate asked her, "No queens?"

"Years ago, south of here in Hallapoosa, there was a personable colored lady of considerable size, who, beneath a delicate lace parasol, high-step strutted ahead of a five-piece band at funeral marches. Wasn't nobility, but called herself Queenie Parade."

110

"You never wear purple," he said.

"Not often. Yet in my closet hangs a faded purple bathrobe—with matching slippers—that I slip on whenever I'm longing for a certain bus."

"Purple when you're feeling blue?"

"Oh, that's natural."

"Let's seal a bargain, Aunt Vidalia. If ever you're feeling blue, visit me, and I'll do likewise."

"It might be more civil," she said in her diplomatic tone, "if you simply knock at my door instead of using your baseball bat to bash souvenirs."

Returning to his chair, he moved it a few inches closer to hers and then sat. "That bat attack," he confessed, "was childish."

"Yes, but do forgive yourself, Mr. Tate. We are to be forgiving, according to our magnificent Nazarene. Perhaps we should also forgive our own debts. It's preferable to guilt or lashing ourselves like monks."

"I'm stymied and boxed in."

Vidalia nodded. "That's very understandable. However, to brighten both our lives, I'm going to tell you a wee secret. My little plan."

"About what?"

"My motive, and your motivation. I am seventy years old. We elderly Southern ladies, in our quiet manner, can be slyer than vixens. Don't let the wafting mimosa fool you. We work our wiles."

"How you do manipulate A.B. whenever it furthers your cause. He and I are helplessly wound around your finger, no

111

more than strands of your knitting yarn."

"Cleverly put. Which leads us to the prime project, and it begins by my asking you to do your aunt Vidalia a favor."

"Name it."

"Years ago, Cappy bought me my first book, *Cash Boy*, by Mr. Horatio Alger. I read it a hundred times. Inside this house, I've been through over half of our comprehensive library."

"Do you want another book?"

Vidalia nodded. "Yes, indeed. I truly do."

"By whom?"

"You."

"Me?"

"Please perfect your writing talent. Hone it sharp. Miss Prudence wrote nice poems, composed well, yet you're far better at it. More tangible. She favored emotion, while you show me *stuff*, objects, things a reader's mind can photograph and keep."

"Oh, you want me to become a *writer*?" His voice hardened nearly to hatred. "Of course, because I'm a cripple. Is that it?"

"Tut." She pinched his hand. "Your mind is sound, Tate Bannock Stonemason, not hamstrung. Use your *strength*. Existence has never been anyone's picnic. There's a burden on every burro. Uphill. But beware of self-pity." She smiled. "We darkies call it *the blues*."

Staring at her, Tate's eyes were mirrors of his own doubt. "You and A.B. both masterminded this con?"

"Wrong. He has no idea. Before you were born, I went to a stationery store and purchased pads, pens, paper, to tell the tale of Ethiopia's Clowns. Alas, I couldn't master it." She reached for his shoulder. "But *you* can."

"The whole story?"

"Every ball, strike, and bus ride. I'll supply the cane, and you'll refine the sugar." A sudden enthusiasm rushed within her, and her finger tapped her temple. "It's all here. Crowd noise, a loud corny band, the smell of a boiled hot dog and the tang of mustard and relish. Strawberry ice cream. The dirt, grass, and a cow in center field."

"You look resolved."

Her jaw tightened. "Mr. Tate, I made you a player, and I ain't through. I'm promoting you from athlete to author, and pointing you toward the Baseball Hall of Fame."

"A *writer* in Cooperstown?"

"You betcha. It wasn't named after any spitting shortstop. Instead, for an author of note, Mr. James Fenimore Cooper."

"Well, I'll be damned."

"Surely you shall be, if you fail to write our story. Now lean neighborly and give Aunt Vidalia a sweet kiss on her cheek."

Immediately after he did so, Vidalia couldn't resist bursting into song, her voice clear and confident:

"Give me . . .
A kiss to build a dream on . . .
And my imagination . . .
Will fly to Cooperstown."

113

They both laughed.

"Where," he asked, "have I heard that? For certain it's one of your olden goldies, or whatever you call them. Who sang it?"

"Satchmo."

Tate winked. "Is he the guy they called Satchel?"

Playfully, she poked his ribs.

BOOK III

ABBOTT

16

"THANK YOU, OLIVER."

Touching his cap's visor, the chauffeur said, "We are home, Mr. Abbott. Been a lengthy trip." He held the Bentley's door.

"Tomorrow is Saturday, so you and I can relax. Ah, but come Sunday, you'll be driving my daughter to church."

"You be right, Mr. Abbott. Miz Vidalia don't cotton to miss a Sunday of Scripture. And I also attend."

Admiring his white manor house, tinted a pale coral in the evening twilight, Abbott Bristol Stonemason felt the quieting balm of returning home. "Good to be back, eh, Oliver? Cozy in Callahoochee."

"Home," said the driver, "is a wondrous word."

A.B. waved a grateful hand as Oliver drove along the white-stoned driveway to a six-car garage, around to the rear. I am blessed, Abbott thought, walking up steps toward the double doors of forest green, to have had the loyalty of Oliver Smith for thirty-five years.

Though the Bentley's roomy backseat was luxuriant comfort, the toll of today's trek tortured his spine. Abbott almost whimpered. Yet he refused to fly. No more! The word *airplane* made him wince.

"Thank you, Frederickson."

Hardly had the houseman opened the doors for his entry, when he saw Tate unevenly walking to greet him, and Abbott's spirit was reborn.

"Great-Granddad, welcome back. How's Jacksonville?"

"Too distant."

"With whom did you confer up north?"

"Republicans. Mostly bankers and financiers. One of them, who wore those yuppie flowered suspenders, actually asked me why I was a Democrat. Not bothering to explain that the late jurist the Honorable Jackson Royster Stonemason was also one, with extremely influential Tallahassee connections, I gave a curt reply. *Because I like living like a Republican.*"

Tate relieved him of his briefcase. "I'll carry that."

"My second meeting was with our associates in the commodities market, which, by the way, is older than the New York Stock Exchange."

"I've never understood futures."

"Few do. Futures aren't as iffy as the public fears, and serve a neutralizing function. May I give you an example?"

"Shoot."

Loosening his necktie, A.B. said, "A pig farmer wanting to sell pork bellies, that's bacon, to Mr. Hormel, is only a tiny tip of the iceberg. Commodities are mainly bought and sold

118

by speculators, none of whom have any intention of either making or taking delivery. Because traders—speculators—so vastly outnumber pig producers and meatpackers, the market becomes more liquid."

"Then it's the army of traders who neutralize and make pork prices stable. And less volatile."

"Bull's-eye."

At times, Abbott was thinking, Tate communicates as an adult. Having spent so much time among sophisticated seniors gave both Prudence Grace and Tate a certain flair. Yet the boy ought to see his friends. But, since the accident, he's never invited a young contemporary to visit here.

Taking his elbow, Abbott guided Tate toward the library. "Can't wait to unbutton my vest and kick off these oxfords," Abbott said a sorry word. "My foot's developing a bunion."

"You can name it Paul."

The humor pleased A.B. A sign that the tensions within Tate Bannock Stonemason could be abating, like an over-tightened violin string lowering in pitch. Once seated in the library, the pair were met by Frederickson's smile and an offer to mix a libation.

"First, why doesn't Vidalia join us? Viddy!"

Pressing an index finger to his lips, Tate signaled for quiet. "She and Ballerina are curled up on the music-room sofa, deep asleep. We dined together, and Cook promised to leave two cold plates in the fridge for you and Oliver."

Abbott kicked off an untied shoe.

"He and I braked for a bite in Orlando, at a Lake Buena Vista hotel. Can't recall which. All lookalikes, clones, and packed with toasted-pink Yankees in flip-flops and T-shirts that say *Kiss Me, I'm from Michigan* over a shiny slathering of baby oil." He turned to his butler. "Frederickson," Abbott said, "please pardon our keeping you waiting. What can you serve an ancient nomad who motors because he's recently become too jittery to fly?"

"Considering the late hour, Mr. Abbott, and as whiskey might disturb your sleeping, I'd suggest a dram of light sherry." His face brightened. "A dry amontillado as a lullaby."

Abbott pouted. "No bourbon?"

Using an affable cough as a reprimand, the butler said, "Miz Vidalia, sir, has requested not to encourage bourbon except before dinner."

"You can inform *Miz* Vidalia that she isn't yet," Abbott growled, "the concierge in charge of *me*." He grunted out of a second shoe, tempted to throw it. "And I shall order a knockback of sourmash if I choose." Then, after consideration, he said in a subdued voice, "I'll have the sherry."

"And," asked Frederickson, "will Mr. Tate also be having a sip of amontillado?"

A *sip*? Abbott was feeling manipulated. In good faith, of course. A price one pays at eighty-two, to be pampered. The nerve! But then fatigue washed over him like a nighttime coverlet, cozying the mental snuggle into a contentment of being home, a haven where he was coddled by both kin and staff. Well, why not? He needed them far more than booze.

"Jacksonville," he sighed, "is almost to Georgia."

"During your career," Tate said, "no doubt you made scores of car trips to Georgia and forgot most of them. Or all."

They were served their sherry in diminutive crystal snifters, aptly selected by the butler as a perfect size for so unpresumptuous a drink.

"Ah, jolly fine, Frederickson. Thank you. It's late, so please be dismissed. Let's all snooze a bit later tomorrow, especially you and Oliver. Good night."

"Good night, Mr. Abbott." To the sixteen-year-old, he added a cheerful, "And to you, Mr. Tate."

Tate gave him a thumbs-up.

"Oh," said Abbott hurriedly, "before you leave, Frederickson, I have heard the pleasing news, from Viddy, about your daughter's acceptance into graduate school. Congratulations to Hyacinth from all of us."

"Thank you, Mr. Abbott."

Perhaps because it felt so good to be home, the sherry tasted warmingly tart. After a reserved swallow, Abbott set the glass down to study his great-grandson. "Years ago, I had a hankering for college but never got to go." His fingers drummed his knee. "Now what were we discussing?"

"Georgia."

"Yes, and myriad trips north to peaches, pecans, and brilliant U.S. senators." Nodding approval, Abbott raised his voice, hoping that Vidalia would take note. "And every man jack was a staunch Democrat!"

Tate grinned. "The peaches or the pecans?"

"Tut. I'm too tired to be twitted."

"Pardon me, but you didn't seem too wiped out to tease Aunt Vidalia. She's a Republican to taunt you, as you're an atheist to pester her."

"It's a free country. Viddy's an independent thinker, and if she so chooses, can become a tree worshiper." Abbott unbent a stiffening knee. "Earlier, I was about to expound on futures. But somehow I'm drawn back to Georgia and my first wayfaring to that august state."

"When was it?"

"1961."

"How come you went to Georgia?"

"Two reasons. The first was business. Someday you'll also be traveling to tend the burdening estate you'll inherit. Trusts, stocks and bonds, real property." Abbott didn't mention that in their airplane, five lost lives were heavily insured, plus double indemnity for accidental death. All in all, Tate Bannock would be worth millions. "But right now, let's not delve into commerce. I'm too pooped."

"Okay by me, Great-Granddad. I'm easy. Maybe you'd like to tell me your second purpose for going to Georgia in 1961."

"A compelling second reason, Tate. An errand of the heart to respect someone I'd never met but felt I knew. We both got born rawbone poor, in rural dirt, the proverbial deck stacked against our ever climbing up and out of the ditch. Yet we survived and enjoyed success. Over sherry, would you care for a flashback?"

"Got my ears on. Fire away."

17

THE TINY WHITE CHURCH WAS CHOCK-FULL.

Outside, enduring a breezeless afternoon with an overflow crowd of mourners, Abbott Stonemason had removed his light cream-colored Panama hat. Not because of the July heat, but in respect to someone lying cold in a coffin, who might be revered as the most talented and controversial man ever to play the game of baseball:

Tyrus Raymond Cobb.

Looking around, Abbott noticed the countless cars bearing license plates from dozens of states. Not only sedans. Plenty of the local Georgia folks had come in pickup trucks or wagons pulled by mules; others had walked on sorry shoes or come barefoot.

Beside him, an old, unshaven gentleman in a washed-out overall wiped his sweating neck with a soiled rag.

A woman in a cloth bonnet stood near, her head bowed,

staring down at a laceless pair of man's boots. She sobbed, making no noise, her shoulders quivering for the loss of a local and national champion. Perhaps, Abbott was speculating, this moment, a 1961 summer day near the little Georgia town of Cornelia, would be its most intimate taste of immortality.

The elderly man glanced at Abbott, nodding once, his face betraying no emotion, merely a tacit and reverent emptiness. Oddly, Abbott felt compelled to ask him a quiet question, one probably posed by strangers a thousand times that day.

"Did you know Mr. Cobb?"

"No, not personal," came the hoarse reply from a dry throat. Pointing at his woman, he said, "Emma done. She's distant kin."

"I'm sorry about his going."

The man spoke no more.

Abbott wondered if anyone truly knew Tyrus. How trivial that sportswriters tongue-lashed him in type; so easy to criticize a Cobb, yet not so simple to become one.

During his baseball years, Abbott never played with or against Ty Cobb. Yet he'd met a fellow who had. His name was Jason Tolliver.

"There's never been anyone like him," Tolliver had reported to a group of eager ears, "nor will there ever be. Cobb was Heaven to watch, but Hell to be with. The man was a tapestry of vices. Ah, but once he pulled on his bulky uniform and striped cap, Ty was a Tiger in every sense of the word. Detroit should have spelled it T-Y-G-E-R. To any opposing infielder, his cleats were claws and fangs."

"Dirty player?" he'd asked Tolliver.

"An aggressive one. Best word to describe Cobb would be *intense*. Or *hungry*. Maybe as a boy he had been deprived and growed up so shirttail poor, it appeared to fans that he was trying to catch whatever it was he'd missed having. Clutch it, and allow nobody to steal it away."

Overhead, above the roof of the church, clouds were blocking an unseen sun in a darkening sky, and Abbott thought he detected a distant rumbling threat of thunder. Looking about, he doubted that even a crashing electric storm could disperse this crowd. Whenever the thunder stilled, he heard the muffled words of a minister inside the church. As a boy in Cornelia, or nearby Royston, Abbott mused, had this preacher once played baseball with the deceased?

Inside, the reverend ended his tribute.

A moment later, what sounded to Abbott like a pump organ wheezed into a hymn, as if laboring uphill. A final note was sustained, perhaps as a cue, followed by an assortment of voices, male and female, launching into often-sung notes and phrases, perhaps without hymnals:

> "Rock of Ages, cleft for me,
>   Let me hide myself in Thee;
>   Let the water and the blood,
>   From Thy wounded side which flowed,
>   Be of sin the double cure;
>   Save from wrath and make . . . me . . . pure.
>   Aaaaaaaamenn."

Although not a professional choir, to Abbott's ear, the rawboned voices shyly blended to sanctify the song. The psalm prospered in plainness.

After a woman offered another modest prayer, there was a pause, then a second hymn, *Blessed Assurance.*

Slowly, one by one or in couples, the people vacated the little chapel, shaking their heads as though reluctant to leave. Expressionless faces infrequently mumbled to others. Hands met, or a palm patted a shoulder as if to say, "There, there," to a neighbor.

Not a single parishioner hurried to a car or wagon in order to beat the crowd. All stood in the ponderous heat, patiently waiting for a black hearse to claim a brown coffin. With finality, double doors closed to lead a decorous departure.

As the hearse rolled through the dust, all heads bowed. Hats remained held and no one spoke. Nearby, in a farm field, three black men had been hoeing rows of vegetables. Yet as the hearse passed, every idle hoe was lightly gripped and held vertically, the rounded butt of its handle pointing at a hazy sky.

After the hearse rolled from sight, no one wanted to be first to speak.

Finally, a stocky gentleman in a blue suit slowly lifted his hat to his head. Staring at the man's face, Abbott thought he recognized another baseballer of note, Mickey Cochrane. Was it? If so, nobody was pestering for an autograph, perhaps because this was a time for a solitary star. It was Cobb's day, no one else's.

The three field hands remained standing in rural respect, hoes frozen at their sides, a humble honor guard standing at attention.

A mule brayed.

Eyeing the congregation, Abbott was awed by them. Dignity in denim. Poor people enriched because they'd been contemporaries of a fellow Georgian who, like them, had run on dirty toes beneath their majestic trees of pecan. He belonged only to them, but on this scalding July afternoon in 1961, they fervently belonged to him.

Baseball fans? Not on this day, nor at such a serene site of worship. Miraculously, they all appeared to have been cleansed by coming.

One buried.

All others uplifted.

Abbott Bristol Stonemason had been realizing that his shirt, underneath his suit jacket, was dampened with perspiration. Refusing to remove his coat at the funeral, he forced himself to adjust to the discomfort.

This baseball great had been nicknamed The Georgia Peach; well deserved, as he certainly played a sweet game of ball. Inside, the peach had a pit harder than any nut could be, a pit that, according to his ornery onfield reputation, had cracked more than one tooth. No player ever slid harder into second base, or into a second baseman. Cobb, if he couldn't break up a double play, would at least try to bust up a shortstop.

Walking toward his car, Abbott recalled listening to a particular major-league game on the radio, decades ago. Cobb's team, the Detroit Tigers, was up against the Sox. Because of Cobb and his cronies, the two middle infielders on the Sox wore shin guards to save their legs from Tiger talons.

For certain, Cobb was a spiker.

Yet that wasn't why he deserved respect. For three seasons, Ty had batted .400 or better. His lifetime average was higher than anyone who ever played the game. He topped all stolen-base leaders for six years; best RBI producer for four. And extra-base slugging champ for eight seasons!

If, Abbott was thinking, I had to choose somebody to crown second-best to Cobb, it would be Rogers Hornsby.

It was 1909, Abbott guessed, when a particular middle infielder didn't knuckle under Ty. His name was Honus Wagner. Cobb came sliding into second base on his back, sharpened cleats high. Waiting on him, a bare hand gripping a baseball, Wagner tagged Cobb's head so hard that it knocked him unconscious.

Once again in the blistering heat inside his new Buick, Abbott Stonemason followed the long but patient line of cars, a file of giant motorized ants creeping over the hills of Georgia clay, through Carnesville and toward Royston. All along the route, mourners stood silently in respect, proud to work the soil where a hero was hatched who never failed to revisit and wave hello. Without a Tyrus Raymond Cobb, their children would have no hospital.

The black hearse rolled by them, and for a brief moment in their drab shroud of poverty, they lived in league with a legend.

A peach . . . etched into eternity.

From his saddle-leather den chair, Abbott Bristol
Stonemason glanced over a *Wall Street Journal* to smile at
his daughter, entering the cozy retreat.

"Does our beloved one sleep?"

Vidalia nodded. "*Erased,* as he would say. Likewise my
dog." Sitting primly on the other side of a cherrywood coffee table, she lifted her teacup, then paused. "You and poor
old Ballerina hiked him out this afternoon, and thank goodness you did. His tantrum surely exhausted me."

"Frustration voltage," A.B. said. "Tate's become a one-
legged topiary tree, top-heavy with mental distress, threaten-
ing to topple."

"Or a grenade. Pin pulled." Vidalia bit her lip. "We're
helplessly counting the seconds prior to his next explosion."
After a sip of tea, she added, "We can't save his leg. But
somehow, we must rescue his mind."

Removing his glasses, Abbott rubbed his eyes. "Whatever shall we do, Viddy? How will we refocus him? I'm eighty-bloody-two! Well beyond a decade I've been semiretired, easing myself out of Stonemason Enterprises and into carpet slippers."

"A deserved rest."

"Had it all entirely planned. Charles, my astute grandson, was firmly entrenched as CEO, with ample backup, as Amelia was a competent executive as well as a charming wife. Jackson's legal acumen was legion, contacts galore, and His Honor's wife, Dolly, was a real-estate genius. Following college, Prudence Grace Ann planned to join our management."

Rising, he strolled to the east window to stare blankly at the expansive lawn's towering live oaks and their massive twisted limbs, curving from the trunks like wooden pythons.

Somewhere, deeper into the starlit night, a lonesome whippoorwill persisted in repeating his name.

"Gone," he whispered. "They're all gone, Viddy. But luckily I still have *you*." Turning, then forcing a grin, he added, "I'm even more grateful that, at last, you've been given what you always wanted. A child to raise."

Her eyes softened. "You know?"

"For a long spell I have known. Scores of years. Your silence, Vidalia, never fooled us. Lavinia and I were quite aware."

Viddy looked down at her hands. "Father, I felt so compelled to offer a child wholesome parentage, plus advantages I never had. Alas, I was childless. Barren by choice."

"We assumed. Denied what you most desired, you

remained a spinster, donating all those years of caring to Jackson Royster, my son and your kid brother. Then to his one heir, Charles Boyd, going a step further and selecting a superb wife for him." He pointed at her. "Oh yes, I know Miss Amelia Booth Bannock was your personal pick of a litter of lovely lasses. And the brace of you, conniving in cahoots, double-teamed my grandson Charles down the aisle."

Vidalia nodded. "Guilty as charged."

"There's more. Prudence Grace Ann came along, whom you cornered as your Barbie doll, coaxing her into teeth braces when no one else could. And shopping with her for cotillion frocks."

"On prom night, how could one *not* adorn Miss Prudy? I was a fairy godmother primping my Cinderella, our private joke, to be the belle of the brawl." Her face contorted. "I can never get over our losing Prudence Grace."

"Nor I."

They both stayed quiet for a long moment. Abbott, to lighten their mood, said, "Viddy, your maternity and maturity parented my entire family, as your little girlhood mothered all of your Clowns."

"One does one's best."

"And then, finally, your long-awaited dream boy: Master Tate Bannock Stonemason." Abbott stepped closer to her. "My dear daughter, never from your own loins could you have birthed a baby whose essence was your echo." His voice lowered. "Now, more than anyone's, as the pair of you huddle together to exchange secrets, Tater has become *yours*."

131

"For such a professed atheist, you also can be the epitome of empathy."

"What I am matters not. Only an aging great-grandfather. A relic. Ah, but you, my dear Viddy—" Abbott howled— "you're now in the prime of life. Hah! A seventy-year-old *mammy*."

She offered a slight bow. "You'll pardon me, I hope, if I don't shuffle, tap dance, or sing *Shortnin' Bread*."

"Viddy, my dear, I guess you and I are not retired, or washed-up, as we previously assumed. Our game's still going on."

"Ain't over until Yogi Berra sings."

It took Abbott a second or two until her jest jolted him. They both enjoyed the humor. Sinking again into his leather chair, he waited for its cushion to cease hissing. "We needed a lick of laughter."

"Really."

"Viddy, six months ago, I wasn't prepared for that dreadful accident. Nor ready to resume the reins of our corporation, so comfortable was I waxing and withering into—let me find a suitable term—a benign senility."

"You are neither benign nor senile. If I may express a considered opinion . . . "

"That's a hoot. Your two cents are seldom omitted. I recall you at ten, hadn't lived with Lavinia and me a week even, and you rearranged every item in your room."

"Naturally." Vidalia smiled. "It's a female eccentricity called *nesting*. You, a bird fancier, have seen a mother wren pulling a twig from one rampart of her nest, poking it somewhere else. Men don't understand this phenomenon."

"We don't?"

"No, it's too artistic for a masculine mind. Remember the fuss you kicked up when Mother wanted the piano moved? Men can't abide a domestic reshuffle, yet women crave it. Thus, as a child, I shifted my twigs to suit me." She sighed. "I sought a new life because I so deeply missed my Clowns."

"How rarely you mention those teammates by name. Leastwise," he said, "not that I recall."

"Some memories are too personal to be made public, but should be kept under lock and key, in a diary of the heart." Vidalia suddenly slapped her knee. "It would be tempting, however, to tell you how Tater and I stayed up all night together a week ago."

"Let's hear."

"You were snoring like a chainsaw calling to its mate. But your great-grandson swung a baseball bat, bashed his trophies, and then, an emotional wreck, he disintegrated into my arms."

"What happened, Viddy?"

"Tate and I brewed tea and sat in the porch rockers to talk." She paused to reflect. "No, I talked. More than hearing, Tate absorbed, on a subject you and I have so gingerly been dodging."

Abbott felt his mouth open. "Baseball?"

Vidalia nodded.

"Quite a coincidence. Because recently, I told him about my attending Ty Cobb's funeral. So, you people also jawed about baseball."

She shrugged. "That, and a bite of sociology, as I told him about a wee mote of a mascot. And how two veteran baseballers, gray and grizzly, cared enough to braid her hair and scrub mud from between her toes."

"So long ago that it resurrects little, except how old and rusty I have become."

"And I. But we cannot dwell upon ourselves. Better to herald our good fortune." Leaning forward, she said, "Father, we are reborn! The two of us are now Tater's age. We're sixteen again."

"Can we tackle it, Viddy?"

"We have no choice. An exploding Cessna has recaptured our youth. And with every gift there comes a concomitant duty. Responsibility ain't no load of feathers."

"Good grief. You and I into brooding?" Abbott shook his head. "A bouncing brood of one."

"Yes!" Eyebrows lifted, her chin elevated an inch or two, and eyes that could dissolve granite penetrated him. "How blessed we are. For years, sir, you and I have been coasting in neutral, inert, slipping into a comfortable shawl of seniority, accepting the homage bestowed upon us by younger generations and their *kinder*. Here we sat, Father, enthroned in a court of antiquity."

His fist pounded the chair arm.

"God, I hate it whenever you confounded Republicans attempt to be intellectual."

"Rot. You revel in it. You bloom whenever any Stonemason manifests a capacity to reason. Logic fascinates you. You clap whenever one of us thinks abstractly."

"How so?"

Holding up three fingers, Vidalia said, "You told us that intellect is a pyramid of three tiers. At its base, groundlings, as you and Shakespeare call them, mainly discuss *people*. The mediocrities, *events*, like a Super Bowl. But at the apex, the brainy elite debate *concepts*, ideas, and their structure."

At times, Abbott was in awe of his adopted daughter. How articulately she could sum up what he had, perhaps, merely mumbled.

Perception, discovered in a dugout.

"However," he said, imploringly opening his hands, "we digress. Returning to our riddle of the moment, we have a tempestuous man-child to raise. Damn it."

Rising, she walked slowly to behind his chair, leaned over, and with a hand resting on his shoulder, she kissed his cheek. "You and Tater," she said. "Inside, you're each lighter than a moth."

"Bless you, Daughter," he whispered. "Thanks, eons ago, for adopting my sweet Lavinia and me."

"Best we put aside our past. The game isn't over, A.B. Weary we are, yet you and I are still suited up to trot back out on that diamond and play."

"Play?"

"Extra innings."

"TATE," HE CALLED TO HIS GREAT-GRANDSON, "YOU MIGHT find this unusually fascinating, so come and check it out."

Waiting for Tate and Ballerina to approach, A.B.'s observation became an instant comparison: Tate's walk appeared stronger, but the dog could barely move. For her, hiking had become an unsteady hobble when pain accompanied every step.

"Easy," he warned. "Hold the dog, please, so she doesn't inadvertently disturb what you're about to see." Abbott slowly pointed at a brown blanket of leaves on the ground. "Look there."

"It's a snake," Tater said, "eating something. I don't know exactly what kind it is, but I wager you do. And I'd like to learn."

"Yellow rat snake. They're not in the least poisonous, but kill by constriction. As you see, the jaws are unhinged, allowing it to devour a careless rabbit fawn. Years ago, as a lad, I kept a yellow rat snake for a pet."

With a wink, Tate asked, "Couldn't get a girl?"

"Of course. Later in life there were ladies aplenty, as I was considered to be quite dapper."

"You still are, Great-Granddad."

Pressing on, they passed through endless stands of brown-top millet, plus some green and yellow citron. In days past, Ballerina had usually scampered ahead to quarter a field, wisely staying within gun range, nosing the golden switch-grass for quail or chucker partridge. A joy to hunt with, motionlessly locking to a hard point whenever she'd scented a bird.

No longer.

Abbott noticed the coonhound's uneven fatigue, a mind-less plod, her sagging head informing him that she felt little joy in travel.

Only a grinding grip of age.

Respecting her, wanting to scoop the hound into his arms, Abbott accepted that he could no longer take the animal home to Viddy. Today would mark an end to Ballerina's life.

Instinctively, his hand sought the holstered Ruger that was belted at his waist. Earlier, Tate had asked about the pistol. He hadn't honestly answered, deflecting the boy's curiosity with an evasive remark about a prevalence of possum and raccoon.

"Varmints," he'd grunted, hoping a single grumpy word might abort the lad's further interrogations.

Leaving the snake to its prey, they moved on.

"We haven't been in this section of property, have we, Great-Granddad? If so, I don't recall this place."

"There's a reason."

"You're sounding a bit secretive. In fact, all afternoon you have been somewhat preoccupied. Are you deep in thought?"

Abbott stopped. "We're on a mission," he said. "One of mercy. Viddy knows. For a few days now, she and I have been discussing the inevitable, how to handle it with compassion and dignity."

"Please wait up, Great-Granddad. You're walking too fast for either Ballerina or me to catch you."

Turning, he looked at the boy, then slowly raised an arm to a level pointing. "Back yonder, a rat snake is dining because it happened to be the time for a rabbit to die. Every human has to face death, as do all creatures." Abbott hauled in a deep breath. "Today is also Ballerina's time."

"Now?"

"Soon. Up ahead."

Tate approached to stare straight into his great-grandfather with sober blue eyes that already knew and understood. Never had Abbott seen Tate Bannock Stonemason appear so full-fledged. How ironic, this day of mixed blessing.

"So that's why you brought the Ruger."

Abbott nodded.

"You're intending to shoot her."

"No. You are."

"Me?"

"You. Because I have homed and hunted with her for a decade. We can't ask Viddy to perform this, yet, having discussed it, I know we have her reluctant approval. As you're the stocky bull calf of our herd, you are nominated." With a gentle hand on a young shoulder, he asked, "Can you do it?"

"Yes," Tate said without hesitation. "Because it has to be done. You and Aunt Vidalia aren't the only cognizant people. I've noticed. And it's heartrending to watch Ballerina falter. If I call her name, she doesn't always hear. And when a chair is relocated, sometimes she'll bump into it. Every step hurts. Her moaning is a plea for help." Tate swallowed. "One of us ought to rescue her."

"It's a lot to ask of you, Tater."

"She's a lot of dog."

"Okay, let's continue. Ahead there's soft earth and a shovel, hidden in a certain place for this purpose. It means you'll have to dig a grave. I can help."

"No. Allow me to handle the entire task. Because it's time I hauled some family freight. After all, soon I'll be seventeen, and countless young men my age are already married, supporting a wife and child." He nodded. "Trust me, Great-Granddad."

Looking at Tate with a growing pride, Abbott said, "Yes, I believe you'll cut it."

Resting on a fallen log, Abbott stroked Ballerina's silken spine, alarmed at how thin she'd become, feeling ribs. Together they watched Tate scoop out a grave, shoveling black Florida muck onto a lighter surface sand.

"There." Tate leaned on the shovel. "Easy part's finished." He walked to them. "Now, if you lend me your pistol and walk away, I'll end our friend's suffering."

Though sounding grown-up, the boy bit his lip.

Drawing the revolver, Abbott said, "It's a .22 caliber frontier-style six-shooter. Single action, which means you have to cock it by working back the hammer with your thumb." He took a breath. "One bullet in the back of the head will do."

"What if I only wound her? I wish we'd brought that Army .45."

"Needless overkill, and also dangerous. Why employ a sledgehammer to drive a thumbtack? Passing through the dog's skull, a .45 slug might continue and ricochet into you, or me, and cut us in half."

Handing the pistol to Tate, he knelt to caress Ballerina a final time. His hand could barely pull away from the warmth of her head. Fists clenched, he walked away.

Abbott waited.

After an eternity, he slightly flinched at the sharp bark of a Ruger's report. Just one. No second sound. In ten minutes, Tate appeared and walked toward him, arm hanging, pointing the pistol at the ground.

"I replaced the shovel where you'd hidden it." His voice was shaky. "Yes, and also wiped its blade clean of all dirt."

"You're becoming manly, Tate Bannock."

"Finally. It's taken time."

"When we arrive home, Tate, I shall expect you to swab the bore clean and then add a drop of oil. We who discharge firearms must also engage in housekeeping."

"Will do."

"By the way, thank you. Forgive my doubting that you'd have the backbone to do what I couldn't."

Together, they walked toward the manor, side by side, in stride. Abbott was wondering how many deaths he could endure. As of late, Vidalia hadn't been acting too perky. Oliver, he'd learned, was taking her regularly to consult a heart specialist.

"How," Tate asked, "do we tell Aunt Vidalia?"

"Oh, that perceptive woman will merely study our faces and read a complete story. She can weather Ballerina's death. However, if both you and Prudence Grace had died in our Cessna, I believe Viddy might have crumbled."

"Soon as we're home, I'll want to see her."

Abbott nodded. "As will I."

THEY RETURNED BY A BACKYARD PATH.

Nearing a rainbow garden of blooms and butterflies, Abbott heard the familiar *clack clack clack* of a brightly painted whirligig. A breeze caused its small wooden pro-peller to spin and a tiny red-shirted farmer to whack a tree stump with an axe while his dog jumped.

Years ago, Vidalia had positioned it there, high on a pole, to intrigue generations of young Stonemasons.

Beneath it, there she stood on this sorrowful afternoon, filling a bird feeder with seeds, no doubt awaiting their return. As usual, she wore an inexpensive dress of bleached white cotton, plus a sunbonnet. Seeing her caused both Abbott and Tate to foot-drag a step, until, noticing them, she waved a gloved hand.

Three had departed for a hike, yet only two came back; thus there was no halting question to be asked or answered.

142

Nearing her, the two men wordlessly stopped.

She touched Abbott's arm and Tate's.

"I gave Cook an afternoon and evening off," Vidalia told them, "so I could contrive a homely little supper, just for family. Perhaps I'm in need of caring company."

Rather than in the formal dining hall, Vidalia had set a table for three in what was called a nook, adjacent to the butler's pantry. At first, there was scant conversation except for Abbott's and Tate's endorsements of the fare. Catfish, collard greens and vinegar, hot buttery grits, cucumber, slices of gumbo okra, crisp sprigs of fresh parsley, tomato wedges, iced tea with lemon or lime, plus a few oval leaves of her herb garden's mint.

For dessert, a pint-sized shortcake, slightly toasted brown and still oven-warm, as a refuge for crushed Plant City strawberries.

"Aunt Vidalia," said Tate, wiping a drop of berry juice from his chin, "you are a classic cook, as well as being a stately Southern belle. And you make Stonemason Manor a Tara."

"Thank you, Mr. Tate, but please don't overstate my kitchen ken." Her face lifted in jest. "Look close, and you'll not see much scarlet."

They all enjoyed a pun.

"I'm hankering," she softly added, "to see another young Mrs. Stonemason residing here, before too many years."

In mock annoyance, Tate looked at her. "Miz Vidalia, are you blueprinting my life?" He sighed. "I hope so, as it begs counsel."

"Not to butt in," Abbott butted in, "but Viddy and I only want you to grow prosperous in mind and spirit."

"What a relief to realize," his great-grandson retorted with a grin, "that the pair of you have prefabbed my life, boiled it, and poured it into your selected mold. What am I? Jell-O?"

"No," said Abbott, "you're merely ours."

Upon saying the word, he glanced at his daughter, and their eyes briefly locked. *Ours*. Sixty years ago, he'd uttered that one precious word to Lavinia, admitting he couldn't offer Vidalia to any other family.

Alas, it was so long ago, perhaps during the Crusades. "That's the trouble with old age," he muttered to no one in particular. "It lasts too cussed long."

Smiling at his great-grandson, he said, "To you, Viddy and I are petrified fossils. However, lately we have been honored by a bounty that is, to us, beyond Magi proportion. You. Tater, we aren't gods, but merely two denizens of decrepitude, determined to nurture you toward Providence."

"Rhode Island?"

"No, witty one," said Vidalia. Lovingly, she touched his hand. "All we expect, Mr. Tate, is that you become another Robert E. Lee."

After a swallow of iced tea, Tate said, "By the way, Aunt Vidalia, I'm within a few pages of finishing the book you lent me, about General Lee." He thoughtfully nodded. "Quite an accomplished fellow. A pity he was never our president instead of either Lincoln or Grant."

"Amen," said Abbott. "Lee might have prevented a disastrous war that killed or crippled almost a million soldiers."

"I quite agree," Vidalia stated. She started to rise from the table. Unable, she wobbled a step, leaning against the door-jamb in an attempt to steady herself.

"Viddy!" Abbott almost choked. "What's wrong?"

"Nothing . . . nothing . . . "

"Tate, please take one side of her while I brace the other. Today's been a strain on us all—mostly on Vidalia, I'm afraid."

"I just felt a bit faint, that's all. I shall be all right, so you people don't need to mollycoddle."

"What we are going to do," Abbott said, "is escort you directly upstairs and to your bedchamber."

"I've got her, Great-Granddad."

"Good lad. We mustn't let her fall. She appears to be a bit woozy."

"Please don't make a fuss. I haven't had a woozy day in my entire life," Vidalia insisted. "It just might have been those collards. I relish them so much, yet sometimes they challenge my digestion."

Holding her wrist, Tate studied his wristwatch. "Please, everyone hush for a few seconds."

Abbott waited.

"Well," the boy announced, "her pulse seems relatively normal." He grinned at Abbott. "Mine's racing like Richard Petty."

"Mine too," Abbott told him.

"Shall we chaperon her upstairs?"

Abbott nodded. "Yes, but please, let's not hurry it. After all, there's no reason to panic. None at all." Then, to be positive, he allowed himself a wisp of wishful thinking. "Vidalia's healthier than a hinny."

Slowly and solicitously, the two of them sandwiched Vidalia away from the butler's nook, through the spacious foyer, then up the long and curving burgundy-carpeted staircase. Several times they stopped, checked on her, then continued. No one spoke until the trio finally attained the top step and steered in the direction of Vidalia's room.

"Great-Granddad . . . "

"Yes?"

"I can't stand it any longer. What's a hinny?"

Almost laughing, Abbott warned him. "Tate Bannock, at times you really exasperate my disposition. Gad, during such a moment of stress, is that all you can think about?"

"I'd like to know, too," Vidalia said.

"A few minutes ago, downstairs," Abbott grunted, "I was fixing to telephone 911 for an ambulance. Right now, I'd hazard that what the three of us ought to summon is a shrink."

Tate giggled. "Is that like a hinny?"

"Sort of. A hinny's the converse of a mule," Abbott said. "A jackass and mare produce a mule, while a stallion horse to a jenny ass begets a hinny."

"Of course," Tater said, rolling his eyes. "That certainly would've been my first guess."

They continued along the hall, laughing, enjoying one another. Abbott felt slightly relieved that Tate, in his inimitable boyish manner, had somehow eased their mood of concern.

At last, Vidalia was comfortably stretched out on a soft

and inviting bedspread, her white hair in repose upon a lavender pillowcase. She gazed up at Abbott on the side of the queenly four-poster, then at Tate on the other.

"My, what gallant nursing. Thank you."

Disappearing for a moment, Tate returned, clanking a small cowbell. "Here," he said, "I'll leave this by your bedside. Rattle it anytime of the day or night, and I'll come bookin'. Okay?"

Vidalia nodded. "I feel better already."

"Good," Abbott said. As Tate removed her shoes, then covered her with a light summery blanket, Abbott asked, "Is there anything you require? Whatever, we'll fetch it up here to you, jolly smart. Vidalia, are you sure there's nothing you want?"

Holding hands with both of them, she looked up at Abbott. "Yes, there's one thing. Something I've wished and hoped for a number of years."

"Name it," Abbott said, "and it's yours."

"All right. It is something important to me. Urgent, one might say." She paused for a breath. "But you have the right to refuse."

Stiffening his spine, Abbott said, "No, I shall not deny you anything as long as you don't insist on my becoming a Republican. If this request of yours is within my power to grant, you have my solemn *promise*." He waited impatiently. "Well, what is it, Vidalia?"

"I want my bishop to baptize you."

"What?" Abbott winced. "In some infernal *church*?"

"No, in living water."

21

A WEEK LATER, VIDALIA HAD NOT REVERTED TO HER CHIPPER self; she was determined enough, however, to attend a tea.

Another promising sign: Abbott had overheard Tate singing in the shower, something about "*you're my lovin' spoonful.*" Drying off, the boy was actually whistling. Something was afoot. Then, whooping a hurried farewell, Tate departed to stride manfully down the driveway, only slightly limping.

The solemn mass of a Florida afternoon quieted to a humid hush, with none of the usual chip-chip-chipping of cardinals. Not even a lean-tailed mockingbird was rehearsing a repertoire.

As Abbott sat alone at a study desk, meticulously culling a contract and questioning why some attorneys couldn't compose a declarative Anglo-Saxon sentence without an obscure Latin phrase, he heard voices. Two of them! One was familiar, decidedly that of his great-grandson; the other, however, was flirtatiously feminine.

Forms appeared at his door.

"Great-Granddad, mind if we pop in to howdy? I'm sure you remember Angelina?"

In a heartbeat, elation swept through Abbott's mind, almost before he could peer up and over his half-moon glasses to focus. A pair of young people loosely held hands, pinky fingers interlocked. But beyond that, Angelina and Tate seemed to be basking in friendship.

"May we come in?"

"Enter, and welcome!" Abbott nearly vaulted across his desk to greet the callers. "Please march right in. We both are honored by your visit, young lady." He glowered at Tate. "Long overdue."

Her smile was electric, glowing, effervescent with enthusiasm. Mystically, this Della-Rialto girl had inherited Lavinia's pirouetting eyes.

"How, pray tell, is your reverent father? Well, I hope. During my lifetime, I've managed to avoid most doctors, lawyers, and clergymen of assorted denominations. Yet your dad, on the one happenstance we met, was tolerable. A refreshing departure from a few of our local breed of Bible wallopers, whose dual purpose is to convert my will and my wallet."

"For years," Tate explained hurriedly, "we've all tried to pry Great-Granddad out of his muted shell. He's so reluctant to express an opinion."

"Hush!" Abbott cannonaded. "I'm courting a belle who

149

embellishes our presence and waltzes my soul."

Holding out both hands to her, Abbott felt delighted when she confidently clasped them. Good strong mitts, he mused, traditionally having harbored a loathing for women with teacup fingers.

"Is Aunt Vidalia around?" Tate asked.

"No. Went skedaddling off to a social. There's only we three to ballyhoo. Say! I'm tempted to ring Frederickson for a mild refresher."

Still holding his hands, Angelina said, "Mr. Stonemason, if I may say so, sir, you're a colonel of cordiality. More than merely feeling at ease, I'm at home."

"Good. Jolly good. Glad you two could, as Tate might put it, hang." A.B. smiled, pleased that he sounded so hip. Or was it hep? Releasing one of her hands, he turned to Tate. "Please offer our guest a seat."

Before Tate could respond, she asked Abbott, "May I have a choice? There's a special chair I'm itching to try."

"Choose, my dear."

In a whirl, Angelina darted behind his desk and regally sat on the button-pocked highback of red leather. "Ah, I'm perched." She laughed like a lyric. "Pretending to be important."

"You are," Tate told her. "Angie, you weren't born, you were ordained into elegance."

"We," she responded, pushing her nose up with a Victorian fingertip, "are amused."

My great-grandchild, Abbott thought, is in the company of a woman fair and fine. And, I sense, one of fiber. "Tate," he stated, "if you don't court this patrician plum, I shall kneel and propose to her myself. Oh, those ox-brown eyes."

Lavinia reincarnated.

Impulsively, he buzzed for Frederickson.

"Champagne, if you please," he ordered when the butler appeared. "It's merely afternoon, so only a modest bottle, Frederickson. A split. I feel younger than a cherub, so let's strum the harp of happiness. Today's a day worthy of observance."

Frederickson beamed.

"Mr. Abbott," he said softly, "I know of a particular bottle that I've saved for a special time." As the butler glanced briefly at Angelina, his genuine smile appraisingly blossomed with approval. To Abbott, he offered a subtle nod. Only minutes later, spotless white gloves ceremoniously began to uncork and pour the pale golden bubbles into three flutes on a napkin-covered silver tray.

A.B. was first to hoist crystal.

"Miss Angelina Della-Rialto, to you, and also my recovering and resolute great-grandson, Tate Bannock Stonemason, a toast! May you both ripen as grapes in sunlight."

"Hear, hear," Tate said, smiling.

Clink.

The glasses of Tate and Angelina met, ringing as a faint carillon, a celestial chime. Abbott noticed all glasses were still full. None of the three had taken even a wren's sip, perhaps wishing that so restorative a rhythm would endure.

"Pity," he said, "Vidalia isn't here. Today might convince

her to savor a bubble or two of our festivity." Raising his glass, he said, "To us."

They all tasted the toast.

"Someone ought to spout off something scholarly," Tate suggested. "Heavy-duty memorabilia."

As he had a theory about human existence, yet to be expressed, Abbott decided he'd risk taking it out for an airing.

"At birth," he told them, "the unproven artist in each of us is given a large blank canvas. But only one! We have a lifetime to cover its entirety with the hues and textures of adventure, romance, sweat. My mistake was assuming my picture was finished. Wrong. There were extra innings to play. So, approaching eighty-three, I dab on today's colors. Gold and crimson. Paint slowly, both of you, because our errors of oil are not erased. Only when you fill your canvas to the brim can it eventually become your portrait."

The three of them were silent.

After at least a minute, Angelina spoke. "Tate has a handful of brushes. He's taken up new ones." Glancing at her young man, she added, "If you don't tell your great-grandfather, I will."

"Great-Granddad, I've made a decision to go back and finish high school."

"Bully! We are all proud of your recent progress, mental and physical, and I can't wait for this cheering news to bolster Vidalia. In the interim, I suspect she's been tutoring you."

"More or less. We began with my writing a few poems, but then Aunt Vidalia shifted my gears to baseball. Upstairs in my bedroom there's a three-inch stack of notes."

"On her girlhood with the Clowns?"

"Exactly."

"Tater's allowed me a peek, Mr. Stonemason, and it isn't merely a cast of characters," Angie said. "It's a parade with all those unforgettable names, like Junebug, Wash, and Lullaby. The teams, the towns . . . they're a circus, a carnival, and a county fair. It's big-top baseball."

Abbott grinned. "Sort of makes me itching to jump to my feet and cheer for our Callahoochee All-Stars."

"Anyone who reads this story," Angelina went raving on, "will taste root beer, spill mustard, hear a brass band murdering Sousa, pop popcorn, and breathe Americana." She glanced approvingly at Tate. "He plunked me down in a dugout to smell Tonic's hair and touch Cappy's swollen right hand as though nursing it myself."

Tate pretended to punch her.

"Oh, Angie, it isn't anything so dramatic. Not yet." Tate's face sobered into resolution. "But it deserves to be an anthem, not a box score. Part of something more artistic than a ball or a bus."

"Part of what?" Abbott asked, knowing the answer.

"Vidalia's canvas."

22

ABBOTT SWORE.

"Where in Hell did I stow it?"

Earlier, downstairs in his study, he'd yanked open every drawer, even bothering to grope behind a row of books. No luck. Now, upstairs in his bedchamber, A.B. continued the search, pawing through a hodgepodge of souvenirs. Why, he wondered, had he collected such a jumble of stuff?

He knew why. Each trinket represented a boyhood or manhood emblem. Tokens of time.

Locating something else, a yellowing and mutilated photograph, he reunited with it for several minutes, fingers gently clinging to his loss.

"This was taken almost sixty years ago."

In a baggy pair of white knickers, there he stood, leaning on a polished fender of his first flivver, a thirdhand Ford, an arm around Lavinia's wasp waist. A breeze had blown the brim of a flapper hat over one of her eyes. The other eye seemed to be lionizing him, as though he were a matinee idol.

"Lavinia."

Who had taken this picture? Ah, now he remembered: Vidalia, at around the age of eleven, had snapped it.

"Lavinia," he repeated. At times, during their early courtship and marriage, he'd called her Vinny. But that halted because in one household, a Vinny and a Viddy proved too confusing. And to boot, the neighbors had a mongrel dog who constantly strayed and were often calling "Vickie" from their back porch.

The recollection made A.B. smile.

Then, as though tucking away a prologue of his life, Abbott returned the slightly bent photo to its customary tomb. As he closed the drawer, it stuck; then, when he jerked it open a second time in frustration, the object he sought came rolling to the front.

A battered baseball.

"Ah! Here you be, you hunk of horsehide."

It was older than the photograph, and for decades A.B. had wondered why he'd kept it. Now at last he knew the reason, even though, years ago, he'd touched this baseball for less than a second.

Closing the drawer, then rising from stiffening knees with the help of a tormented grunt, A.B. slipped the ball into a roomy pocket of his rumpled plaid bathrobe.

Scuffing along the upstairs hall toward Tate's room, he could hear the persistent *tickety-tick* of a keyboard.

"Still authoring, I see."

Tate looked up. "Great-Granddad? It's close to midnight. Usually at this hour you've already crunched the feathers. Come on in."

Abbott felt tired. Beyond the desk where Tate had been typing, the bedspread looked inviting, so he unceremoniously shuffled over to it, kicked off his carpet slippers, and sprawled.

Tate grinned. "Comfy?"

A.B. nodded. Feeling the bulge in his bathrobe pocket, he produced it and tossed it to Tate, noticing the boy's surprise. "I brought you a present."

"Wow! This is one antique baseball. Have you been saving it since Bull Run?"

"Sixty-five years."

"A homer you hammered to win for the, who were they, the Callahoochee All-Stars? Or was it a circus catch you gloved that saved the game?"

"Neither. Top of the ninth, we were leading by two runs, two away. Runners on the corners. An opposing batter swatted one high and deep. As the left fielder, I easily drifted back, camping under it with my spine against the wall, and raised my glove for a routine snare. Sun blinded me. Although the ball was inches short of the fence, it bounced off my glove, into the bleacher seats, and we eventually lost the game. A three-run homer."

"How did you happen to get the ball?"

"My hometown rooters were booing me, throwing pop bottles. A fan, who'd caught a ball I couldn't, threw it back at me. Having lost a play-off game for my team, standing there, listening to razz, I wanted to lie down and die."

"Did you?"

"Instead, I picked up the ball, the one you're now holding, and later trudged sadly home. Why I saved the ball I didn't immediately comprehend."

"You do now."

"Yes. Because I was nearly kicked off the team in disgrace, yet I survived, married Miss Lavinia Grace Armitage, adopted Vidalia, and begot Jackson Royster Stonemason, who became a judge. Ultimately, I was rewarded by the two finest great-grandchildren a left fielder could ever want."

"Thanks, A.B., for the story and the baseball, mostly for being an ace of an ancestor."

"Over half a century I kept that baseball, to prove to myself that neither failure nor its depression could ever defeat me."

Tater winked. "Got the message."

Abbott studied a boy who, a few weeks ago, he feared he might lose. Soon he'd turn seventeen. A party for four might be in order, one to include Angelina. The family would be born again, refurbished. By dang, speaking of birthdays, Abbott doubted he'd be able to wait to celebrate his upcoming eighty-third.

Tate looked at him.

Abbott returned the concentrated stare, believing how unnecessary words could be whenever affinity passed from one soul mate to another.

Like a baseball.

The night was shattered by an urgent and desperate

157

clanking. A cowbell! As it could only be the one Tate had placed at Vidalia's bedside, both men, neither having an ability for speed, somehow bolted.

They didn't bother to knock.

Lately, at Abbott's insistence, Vidalia slept with her bedroom door slightly ajar, opened about an inch. This allowed Abbott and Tate to dash into the chamber and directly to her bed.

The cowbell abruptly stilled its ringing.

It fell to the floor.

23

TOO EMOTIONALLY SHAKEN TO WALK AWAY FROM AN OPEN grave cradling a handmade pine coffin, Abbott stood alone, unable to leave Viddy.

Her remains had been professionally prepared, with a long white dress, matching shoes and stockings, and a small sky-blue pillow bordered with lace. In keeping with other final wishes, there had been no showy church funeral, neither pomp nor procession. Only family. Plus all of the domestics with whom their revered Miz Vidalia had eaten so many kitchen-table meals.

She called it *soul food*.

The grass neighboring her grave had been thriving for decades, almost as though no one lay beneath the marker. Yet someone did.

Lavinia.

If a man could register anything but sorrow on such a day,

Abbott felt the righteousness of two women, in death, buried side by side. How resplendently Lavinia's face had beamed on the first occasion of Viddy's calling her "Mother."

It hadn't happened right off.

Weeks had passed before their tiny child had even smiled; and then, the most fulfilling of moments: "Mother" spoken in a soft, barefooted hush and with a halo smile.

Considering the two graves, one yawning its bleak and ragged rectangle, the other grassy, Abbott Bristol Stonemason wondered if his ladies were there. Or, as he lifted a chin to the sky, up yonder? There was something eerie in dying that could inspire, he mused, even an aging atheist to contemplate if there was a Heaven.

"No," he rebutted hoarsely, studying all of the graves of departed Stonemasons, his family. "Heaven is here. And I delightedly romped through its flowered garden with all of my angels."

Devoid of purpose, he felt oddly compelled to stroll along the short burial row. One by each, he read the names that remained so clearly in his mind, yet blurred his eyes.

Jackson Royster Stonemason, his only natural child, who had wedded Dolly Madison Tate.

Then their son, Charles Boyd Stonemason, along with his wife, the former Amelia Booth Bannock. Next, their first-born, a daughter named Prudence Grace Ann.

All five, in that exploding Cessna, their charred bodies identified only by dentistry. A curse on that airplane! He hadn't seen it happen, thank goodness, yet his brain had reenacted the scene a thousandfold. On that dreadful day, prior to Oliver's driving them to the airfield, Abbott had heard their laughter, discussing the Braves, the Rockies, and the game of baseball.

Tater's game.

For a while, the boy had been a living tragedy. A leg mangled. A mind soured. And yet, despite his infirmity, this great-grandson forces himself to prance and cavort around the south lawn, holding Angelina's hand.

Even giggling when he tumbles.

"Viddy, you brought him back. You, and later on, Angie." Abbott paused to meditate. "All I requested was to squeeze a bullet into Ballerina." How strange, A.B. was thinking, no longer seeing that loyal coonhound as a sentry outside Vidalia's door.

Empty hall, outside her empty room.

Walking back to her grave, he said, "Toward the end, Viddy, Tate had become your child. And to him you bequeathed your baseball treasury of diamonds. Your extra innings."

Two men with shovels came to the cemetery.

They were both young, in shabby jeans and soiled T-shirts, obviously hired after Vidalia's illness hampered her involvement in domestic selection. These two were the antithesis of Oliver and Frederickson.

A new generation. Hardly new and improved.

They halted to light cigarettes. As he watched, Abbott, who never had smoked, wondered why poor people so often used tobacco. Poor because they smoked? Or vice-versa? No doubt Richard, the head gardener, had sent the pair to return

161

the large pile of loose earth into Vidalia's grave, to cover the coffin. His being there barred them from their job.

"Tate," he said, "where are you?"

No sign of him. Following the final devotions for Vidalia, and Cook's singing *Sweet Hour of Prayer*, his great-grandson had excused himself to depart ahead of the others, appearing hurried, saying, "Great-Granddad, please sort of stand guard here for just a few minutes. There's a thing I forgot. An emergency."

Glancing toward the manor house, Abbott spotted Tate's returning. Yet empty-handed. What could have been so crucial?

"I'm back," he said breathlessly.

"Apparently. Did you have to do something?"

"No. Get something."

When Tate's fist opened to reveal a small item, Abbott squinted. "Hold it still." Stepping a pace closer to Tate, he lowered his face to identify the mystery. An inch in length, it was green and oddly shaped like . . .

"A pickle?" he asked Tate.

"A pin."

"Can't read what it says."

"Heinz."

Abbott was stunned. His memory rolled backward to the game against Ethiopia's Clowns. Their catcher died. A griddle of a day, no breeze, and the old fellow hit a long double, got hung up between second and third, trying for three. His death broke up the team. Their bus wouldn't start, so they left it there and scattered to the winds.

To Tate, he said, "She was wearing that pin on her little washed-out rag of a dress. Barefoot, toes caked in dirt. At home, I scrubbed her feet and ankles."

Oh, he thought, how tenderly I hold that memory. There's something rather sacred in bathing someone else's feet. As one bends and bows to the task, one's soul soars.

Returning to the present, Abbott's fingertips lightly touched the pin in Tate's palm. A last caress.

"She wanted to be buried with it."

"Well, it's too late now," Abbot told him.

"No, it isn't."

Before he could stop the boy, he had climbed down into the grave, pulled the cotter key of the latch, and lifted the coffin lid.

"Tate, do you really want to do this?"

He did it. Closing the lid, he managed to climb out with a bit of difficulty, then noticed the dirt on his hands.

"Want to use my hanky, to wipe?"

"Thank you, no." Tate looked at him squarely, man to man. "If you don't object, for a while I want to keep a reminder of her on me."

Touching Tate's shoulder, he said, "You're turning into quite a stalwart young soldier."

At leisure, hip by hip, they left the small cemetery. Over his shoulder, Abbott noticed the pair of men doing their duty. Pebbles of dirt were hitting pine boards. Each shovelful sounded softer until the sound wafted away to a ghostly silence. Together, A.B. and Tate walked across the broad expanse of manicured St. Augustine grass, thick and bouncy. Not a weed in sight.

"It's proper to keep a promise, Great-Granddad. You made one to her. So did I, that Vidalia's baseball story would be told. My trying to finish it before she died, however, was a bush-league error, as it's not a rush job." He paused. "You know, combing a book, wading into the physical and mental labor, has made me comprehend art."

"Art is our need to be nourished beyond bread. What's your definition?"

"Carving noise into a song."

24

A MONTH PASSED.

In his first tailored suit, a lightweight charcoal, Tate, now seventeen, stood in the shade of the manor's front veranda, already snickering at the upcoming and anticipated event.

A new silver-gray Bentley regally rolled to where they waited. From behind the wheel, their chauffeur hustled to attend a trio of passengers. Holding open a right-rear door, Oliver Smith was flashing a widening smile of satisfaction that bordered on a victorious smirk.

"Morning," he warbled.

Abbott managed a sour nod.

"Good morning, Mr. Abbott, Mr. Tate, and Miss Angelina," Oliver was chirping. "My, my, the Almighty sure bestowed us a blessed sunshiny day for a ritual."

Great-Granddad, however, glowered at Oliver, ducked, grumbled while entering the sedan, and cowered in a

165

backseat corner. Angelina followed, to sit in the middle, then Tate. He felt more comfortable with Angie on his left, beside his strong leg. Weeks ago, when she nudged his mutilated limb, he'd flinch, retreating from her touch. Lately, he had adjusted somewhat, yet still didn't relax.

Intimacy would take time. Impatience, whether his or hers, Tate had concluded, might serve only to ruin two lifetimes. All ought to unfold slowly, like a rosebud.

As the car sedately eased forward and down the sloping driveway to a mammoth wrought-iron gate that was automatically opening, the sulking squire spoke a bit gruffly to his driver. "Since you carried my daughter on countless Sundays, we assume you can locate this . . . this tabernacle."

"Yes, sir. I certain know my way."

"So I fear," Abbott spat. "All three of you best comprehend that, for my part, this sham of a ceremony is neither an act of remorse nor contrition. I'm enduring it to pay a debt."

With a brief squeeze of Angelina's hand, Tate whispered, "He's not as cantankerous as he sounds. Vidalia used to say that all hard-boiled eggs have soft centers." Privately, he hoped A.B. wouldn't kick up too much dust. "There's a chance he'll comply with whatever liturgy the minister performs."

"I heard that," Abbott snapped. "At least you can *pretend* to be on my side, instead of encouraging some Holy Joe."

"Let him steam," Tate said.

Angelina pinched his arm. "Be glad he's still spirited. Plenty of sparkle left in that bottle of burgundy." With a wink, she added, "Fella, ya got good genes in your jeans."

To his left, Tate was noticing out of a corner of his eye, their condemned curmudgeon continued to scowl, immune to frivolity, resigned to his fate as though sentenced to a beheading.

"Right about now," A.B. snorted, "I could dang well use either an anesthetic or a hairy-chested belt of Jack Daniels. With luck, I'll pass out."

Tate wondered if the gentle ewes of the African Blood-of-the-Lamb Baptismal Chapel had been alerted to the rambunctious ram headed their way. Would they stampede in fright?

The Bentley arrived, parking between a freshly painted white church and a surging stream. It took coaxing to pry Abbott from the comforts of his car. He persisted in displaying no interest in the future well-being of his soul.

Over a week ago, Tate knew, Oliver had notified the entire membership that a special guest would appear.

Not quite as momentous as a second Moses descending from the mountain, yet exalted enough to attract not a mere congregation but a crowd. Was every black person in Callahoochee present? It seemed so. Some brought folding chairs for the elderly, plus picnic baskets, even binoculars. After all, a distinguished family's patriarch would be rinsed of sin (and other shortcomings known only to the wealthy), and nobody could forsake a free show. A celebrity! Himself! The very gentleman who'd adopted Miz Vidalia as a tot of ten, taken her in, and given her his name and nobility. Her funeral had been for only family and staff. But today was their opportunity to pay respects to a lady so supportive to this place of worship.

She had even taught Sunday school.

The largest woman Tate had ever met waddled to greet them. As if rehearsed, Oliver handled the heralding.

"Miz Grandiloquentia, I hereby present the fine folks that are close to me like family. Mr. Abbott, Mr. Tate, and Miz Angelina Della-Rialto, whose daddy's a preacher man."

"We thank thee, Brother Smith." Smiling pleasantly, Miz Grand, as she was sometimes known on weekdays, said, "Welcome, Mr. Tate and Miz Angelina. And I 'spect this elder gentleman here is our candidate for absolution, redemption, and overall exculpation?"

The candidate reluctantly nodded.

Turning around, Miz Grandiloquentia announced, "Seems like my husband, the bishop, has momentarily absquatulated." Then her face brightened. "Ah, here comes His Reverence."

Considering the titanic proportions of his wife, Tate couldn't believe that Bishop Ormsby Brimfire Dunkit, as he was known, could be a pygmy. In a rainstorm, His Reverence might seek shelter under a toadstool. He wore, Tate noticed, no shoes or stockings. Nor did several others.

"Assist me!" boomed the bishop.

Without any warning, both Dunkits, large and small, put a hammerlock on an unsuspecting Abbott and, with the help of several substantially built Sisters of the Lamb, promenaded him directly to the river's edge. Uselessly, he struggled, yet into the living (flowing to the sea) water he was dragged, beyond waist deep, flanked by smiling but insistent Lambs.

A.B. finally faced His Reverence, a cleric who wisely stood in a shallower depth.

Abbott, never known for an ability to swim or even the least affinity for wading, screamed in panic. "Tate," he was hollering as though his lungs were made of leather. "Save me!"

"Hallelujah," trumpeted the bishop. "Ye truly wish to be *saved*."

"If'n he don't first freeze to death," Oliver told Tate. "Bishop's daddy baptized me, right out yonder in that ice-cold spring." He pointed. "This particular river water is frigider than Sunday sin."

Grappling against a chilling current, the candidate soon had his fill of religion, having blotted a lifetime supply. Attempting to free himself from restraining hands, Abbott Bristol Stonemason, although the celebrity of the morning, resorted to his only recourse. Profanity. Nothing fancy, just a reliable string of old favorites that spewed forth as a fountain of filth.

Ormsby Brimfire Dunkit, however, could hear only the angels. "Vituperation," he intoned, "shall not behoove ye, Alpert."

"Abbott!" A.B. raged.

Under he was plunged. Repeatedly.

Once for every cussword, which tallied up to a dose of ducking. Baptism, it seemed, was submerging a candidate for every temptation, past, present, domestic, or foreign. The worse Abbott swore, the more His Reverence purified, aided by the beatifying brawn of Miz Grandiloquentia and the Sisters, none of whom were puny. Up, down, up, down, while Abbott continued to demonstrate, between gasps, that a sinner could blaspheme from below as well as above.

Oaths emerged as bubbles.

At last, a soggy and subdued candidate was guided to shore, pumped out and prayed over, congratulated, Lord praised, and wrapped by Brother Oliver in a white blanket. Abbott, who earlier had been eagle fierce, seemed now a half-drowned chicken.

Placing a hallowed little hand on A.B.'s shivering shoulder, Bishop Ormsby Brimfire Dunkit delivered the final humbling benediction.

"Bless you, Alcott."

With a bow, the bishop triumphantly strutted away, perhaps to stamp out some undiscovered impiety. A freshly baptized and devout atheist watched His Reverence's departure, eyes narrowing to slits, opening his mouth to respond with a highly seasoned zinger. Yet nothing came out except a gurgling belch of living water.

Recovering, then slowly confronting his great-grandson, Abbott warned, "Let this be a moral, dear boy. A woman is to honor and cherish. But *never* make one a *promise*."

25

THE FOLLOWING DAY WAS A SONG OF SUNSHINE.

Abbott heard a metallic jingle. Pacing the plush carpet of their library, unable to tranquilize after Vidalia's funeral and that infernal baptism, he pivoted to the tinkling noise, only to see Tate rapidly hobbling toward him.

The lad was itching with eagerness.

"Come on, Great-Granddad." He shook a key ring. "Let's not mope around the house all afternoon. Angie just called, and she's meeting us for . . . consider it celestial therapy. I got the keys to the pickup, so we're off to Apopka."

"Why is she meeting us *there*?"

"For a very uplifting reason." Tate melted Abbott's resistance with a boyishly beaming grin. "It relates to the sky. A wild blue yonder."

As Oliver's elderly Ford clattered away from Stonemason Manor with Tate behind the wheel. Abbott, a bit uneasy, said, "I presume Oliver knows we've taken his truck? Not to bring up mundane details, but do you happen to have a driver's license? Mine expired long ago. One of us ought to have one."

"Got mine a year ago, at sixteen. His truck's the only car Oliver doesn't fret about. He feels I shouldn't practice in the Bentley or anything expensive. Okay by me, because my leg's becoming handy at, as we truckers say, pedal to the metal."

"You're going a bit fast."

"Don't worry. The gas gauge is on E, so we won't be going too fast for very long."

"You certainly build passenger confidence."

"Chill. I was kidding."

After a number of apprehensive miles, they shot through a gate. Abbott, glancing to his left and beyond Tate's profile, tried to read a sign.

TANGERINE
RCACF

"It's a rather unique airfield, Great-Granddad. As a special treat, we are presenting you with a part of the sky."

Abbott stiffened into opposition. "I won't go up. Never! Tate, whatever you're fixing to suggest is in unpardonable taste, considering our family's tragedy." He frowned. "How could you, at this particular time, conjure up so disturbing a prank?"

"Sir, Viddy's funeral is past. We are moving onward, upward, as Vidalia would applaud. For some time, I've been coming here with Angelina, who became interested while I was mending. It was Angie's way of defying the past instead of yielding to it."

"I don't understand, Tate."

"Please be receptive and you shall. Honestly. Back there on the sign, RCACF stands for Remote Control Aircraft of Central Florida. We pilots stay grounded."

"Toys?"

"Small aircraft. A wingspan of five feet, often less. Mr. Fred Hale, who's the chief flight instructor here, is a friend of Angie's dad, and he lets me fly his plane. With supervision." Looking directly at Abbott, he added, "Believe me, my horror of airplanes used to be awesome, so terrifying that I'd scream myself awake at night, drenched in sweat."

Parking beneath a live oak, in shade, Tate dismounted and hobbled around to open the passenger door.

"No." Abbott's face tightened, and he swore. "I won't go near a bloody airplane, or watch. How in the name of compassion could you ask me to?"

"Because we can't cringe forever. Years ago, when I was only eight or nine, you taught me not to flinch at firing a shotgun. Well, it's my turn, A.B., to relieve *your* qualms." He touched Abbott's hand. "Please come, and keep an open mind. You'll be surprised. Trust me. Because I am all you have left to trust."

Hesitantly leaving the truck, Abbott said, "I'm uncertain of my fortitude to stand up to this, boy."

"Be sure, Great-Granddad. Why? Because if I stand up, walk, and even try to run, so can you. You're either a Stonemason or you're not."

To his amazement, in only a few minutes, curiosity led Abbott to examine a tiny red biplane, N 104 BA, belonging to Tate's friend. Peering inside, he detected a quartet of motors that operated four individual functions: the rudder, elevator, throttle, and ailerons, which were wing flaps.

"The fuel," Mr. Hale explained as he filled a tank, "is mostly alcohol, but twenty percent castor oil. Ideal for two-stroke or four-stroke mechanisms. This plane can stay up about twelve or thirteen minutes."

"How high can it fly?" A.B. asked.

"Out of sight," Tate answered. "That's why yellow is so popular, to spot it. Blue, for obvious reasons, would soon be invisible. As to speed, these little bombers can go about a hundred. Want to see me fly one?"

"Well, seeing we're already here . . . "

With augmenting pride, A.B. watched his great-grandson operate a small handheld radio, a transmitter. Its aerial bore a CH 28 chip to establish an exclusive frequency. The miniature plane rolled to their right, cautiously wheeling a one-eighty, then roared by them to a smooth liftoff. Only for a few seconds did its engine emit an exhaust trail.

Once aloft, it was throttled back.

"Now," said Tate, "here's a snap roll. And next I'll do an inside loop, without stalling. But if I nose-dive into an attempted outside loop, the plane will only go so far, then fly inverted. Upside down. See? Get this flat turn, Great-Granddad, using only my rudder. Now a bank, both rudder and ailerons."

"Wow, you're an ace."

"Not quite. Angelina's had me practicing with her plane, a glider. Up there, she'll observe cloud turbulence and locate a thermal, hot air, and make the glider spiral upward, around in circles, and stay airborne for hours. Honest. But gliders don't have landing gear. No wheels."

"Where do they land?"

"Over there, on the grass, so you don't scrape off paint. If you land a glider improperly, on the cement, they call it scratching your ass."

"Charming. Yet apt."

"Whenever a glider coasts in for a landing," Tate enthusiastically explained, "its propeller ought to be horizontal. If vertical, the prop's lower blade might hit the ground and snap off."

"Ah, I see. Instead of being towed aloft, these gliders have an engine. How do you land the biplane you're flying?"

"In the same direction we took off. I'll zoom it to our right and, watch this, dip a wing to a knife-edge bank, reduce power, and float in like cream."

To Abbott's amusement, the biplane lost airspeed and altitude, touching down two main wheels, settling back to tailwheel contact. Slowing, it turned into a short taxiway. When it reached a yellow stop line, Tate cut the engine.

"He's a natural," Mr. Hale joined them to comment. "In our world of miniature aviation, this young man could be another Charles Lindbergh."

"I read about him," Tate said. "The first pilot to fly solo across the Atlantic, but I can't remember when."

"In 1927," Abbott told him, "when I was a kid."

"Cool. I bet that took guts."

Abbott touched the young shoulder. "Took plenty. Courage is a rare commodity, Tate, and you proved your moral courage today. You mustered derring-do to conquer a wounding fear."

Walking back to the Ford pickup, Tate said, "If it's all the same to you, Great-Granddad, I'm not aspiring to conquer anything, or anyone. That's not why I'm . . . flying."

"Why do you?"

"To revel in sunlight instead of wallowing in a pit of grief. And to rid my mind of resenting a handicap that wipes out my hopes of playing baseball." Stopping, he stared at Abbott. "While operating a toy plane, bringing it safely home, I'm not antagonistically out for revenge, to settle a score."

"What *do* you feel, Tater?"

"Not heroic. Nothing at all like Lindbergh or a Yuri Gagarin, but rather like television's Mister Rogers. Am I toe-to-toe with calamity and aching to spit in its eye? Never. Forgiveness is a warm shower."

A car honked!

Then, a breath later, they saw a radiant young Miss Della-Rialto emerge, wearing a white summery dress, to whirl ecstatically once around in the breeze. She waved, yet didn't approach; in a sublime second, Abbott knew why. Angelina stood still, beckoning to Tate with her open and inviting arms, inspiring his smile. The ruse worked.

Without falling, he ran to her.

About the Author

ROBERT NEWTON PECK wrote *A Day No Pigs Would Die*, *A Part of the Sky*, *Cowboy Ghost*, *Nine Man Tree*, and more than sixty other books, including the Soup adventures. Rob plays tennis and ragtime piano, and rapturously lives with his wife, Sam, in Longwood, Florida. His favorite pastime is showing off.